A Note to Readers

While the Fisk and Stevenson families are fictional, James Hill is a real person who headed the Great Northern Railroad. He dreamed of stretching the railroad to the West Coast and worked hard to fulfill that dream, but like many men who headed railroads near the end of the 1800s, James Hill also had a reputation for being harsh toward his workers.

In this book, you'll discover how telephones and electric lights changed people's lives. Like computers today, these new inventions were first used in businesses and gradually made their way into people's homes. Judith and Abe have a hard time imagining a world where every home has a telephone. Can you imagine what it would be like for every home to have as many computers as it has phones?

The American Adventure

LIGHTS
for
MINNEAPOLIS

Susan Martins Miller

BARBOUR
PUBLISHING, INC.
Uhrichsville, Ohio

ISBN 1-57748-289-1

Published by Barbour Publishing, Inc.
        P.O. Box 719
        Uhrichsville, Ohio 44683
        http://www.barbourbooks.com

Member of the
Evangelical Christian
Publishers Association

Printed in the United States of America.

Cover illustration by Peter Pagano.
Inside illustrations by Adam Wallenta.

CHAPTER 1
Emergency!

She ran until her feet throbbed against the pavement. With every step, she wanted to stop, but she could not. She ran until her lungs nearly burst. She ran until her heart could pump no harder. Never in her life had she done anything so difficult. She kept going.

The chilled November air rushed through her nostrils, but she could not get enough of it. Gasping, she forced one foot to go ahead of the other, then the next step, then the next step.

Tangled curly red hair swept in front of her green eyes. She brushed the hair from her face with the back of her hand and kept running. Run, Papa had said, and so she ran through the streets of Minneapolis.

Her father's face hung in the wind before her. His brown eyes were bigger than they usually were, and he did not know what to do with his hands. So he waved his arms around and talked in a loud voice, telling Judith to run.

Papa seemed a lot more nervous than Mama did, even though Mama was the one having the baby. Mama's pains had started quickly. This baby would come fast, just as Judith had eleven years earlier in 1870, and her brother, Walter, two years before that.

Aunt Tina said that Mama was so efficient that she did not have time to waste with a long birth, so she had her babies quickly. Mama was ready for this new baby to come. Papa was acting like he did not realize they were going to have another Fisk child—until the pains started.

Judith had been the last baby to enter her family. For a long time, she'd been the youngest of all the cousins. Then Dr. Dan and his wife, Marcia, had started having babies. Judith remembered when each of them was born. Richard, Anna, and Esther were all still little children. But to have a baby in her own family was new to Judith. She did not know what she should do to help her mother. And after eleven years between babies, her father was not too sure what to do, either. So he had told Judith to run, and she had run.

She pounded the street, dodging people whom she should have been polite to. Later, when they found out why she was in such a hurry, they would understand why she did not stop to chat.

Judith came to an intersection and skidded to a stop. She had to decide which direction to turn. Her chest heaved, and she gulped the air as she considered her choices. A left turn would take her to Aunt Tina and Uncle Enoch's house. Mama was asking for Aunt Tina. She had experience helping other women birth their babies. A right turn would take her to Dr. Dan's medical clinic. Papa wanted his cousin, a doctor, to attend the birth.

"Hey, Judith!"

She spun around to see her cousin, Abraham Stevenson. His shock of dark hair was a welcome sight. She struggled to be able to talk.

"Why are you all red in the face?" Abe asked.

"Am I glad to. . .see you," Judith said gratefully but with difficulty.

Abe scrunched up his face. "Why?"

"I. . .I. . .your mother." Judith tried to fill her lungs.

"Catch your breath and then talk," Abe advised. He kicked casually at a pebble in the street.

"No time," Judith croaked. "Baby's coming."

Abe's brown eyes widened. "The baby's coming? Really? Are you sure?"

Judith rolled her eyes. She was finally able to breathe normally. "Would I be running through the streets like a crazy person for any other reason? Yes, the baby is coming. And my mother wants your mother to be there."

Abe kicked at his rock more forcefully. "It takes you at least ten minutes to run from your house to our house."

"I ran as fast as I could," Judith said in her own defense.

"Of course you did," Abe said. "But why should you have to?"

"There was no streetcar scheduled for another half an hour," Judith answered. "I couldn't wait that long."

"And you shouldn't have to," Abe said.

"Then what are you talking about?" Judith was puzzled—and losing patience. She glanced down the street toward her aunt's house. She was wasting precious time talking to Abe.

"If we all had telephones, your mother could speak to my mother herself. My mother could already be on her way to your house."

"That's well and good," Judith said, "but we haven't got telephones."

"But we could have—if my father were not so stubborn."

"Not very many people have telephones in their houses, Abe," Judith reminded him.

"So what?" he challenged. "We could be one of the first. This is 1881, after all."

"Abe, I would love to stand around and talk about inventions with you, but the baby is coming! I'm supposed to be getting your mother and then Dr. Dan."

Abe gave the rock a solid kick, and it skittered down the street. "You go for Dr. Dan," he said. "I'll send my mother."

"Thanks." Judith immediately turned right and headed for the clinic.

Two minutes later, Abe burst through the back door of the Stevenson house.

"Mama!"

Tina Stevenson appeared in the dining room doorway.

"What is it, Abe?" she asked.

"It's Aunt Alison. The baby's coming."

"The baby!"

"She wants you."

Another form crowded into the doorway. "Did you say the baby is coming?" Abe's sister Polly asked. "Can I come?"

Abraham's mother hesitated only a moment before saying, "Yes, come along. If I know Charles, he'll need some help. He has perfect control over his life—except when it comes to Alison. He hates to see her suffering."

Polly, fifteen years old, pushed fully through the doorway. "What do we need to take?"

"Get the new afghan I just finished," her mother answered. "We'll wrap this baby up in her very own blanket right from the start."

"Her?" Polly chuckled. "It could be a boy."

"I hope it's a boy," Abe said. "With Anna and Esther, we've had enough girl babies lately." Abe wondered if Judith had reached Anna and Esther's father, Dr. Dan.

"Whatever it is, we'll give thanks to God for a safe arrival," his mother said. She turned her head and called out over her shoulder. "Enoch! The baby's on the way. Polly and I are going over to Charles and Alison's."

"Give them all my best," came the muffled reply from Enoch Stevenson's study.

"Get your coat, Polly." Abe's mother turned to him. "I'm afraid you and your father will have to fend for yourselves at supper."

Then she was gone. Abe was left in the house alone with his father, something that he did not like very much. On his way to his own room, he passed the open study door. He paused for just a moment. He knew his father would not look up from the papers he had brought home from the bank.

Being careful to stay out of sight, Abe watched his father from the doorway. The older Stevenson pushed his chair back, leaned on the desk, and pulled himself to his feet. Abe winced as his father limped to the bookshelf, removed a book, and shuffled back to the desk. Everyone always noticed his father's limp. One leg was made out of cork. The real leg had been lost to an injury during the Civil War. The cork leg allowed Abe's father to get around and look after his family. But he never got rid of that shuffle. Everyone knew when Enoch Stevenson was nearby.

Abe went upstairs to his room to wait for news of his new cousin's arrival. He flopped on his bed and picked up the novel he was reading: *Around the World in Eighty Days,* by Jules Verne.

If only they had a telephone!

CHAPTER 2

The Arrival

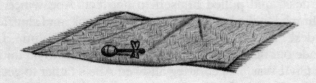

Judith pounded on the clinic's door. She could not believe it was locked. If Dr. Dan was not there and she had to look for him at the hospital or at his house, they would never get back to the Fisk house before the baby was born. She pounded again, then pressed her face against a pane of glass. There were no lights on. The waiting room was empty. It was Saturday afternoon. The clinic was closed.

Turning around, Judith let her weight slide down against the clinic door. She sat on the ground with her legs stretched out in front of her, exhausted. She was not sure she had the strength to sprint off in search of Dr. Dan. Should she go to the hospital, or should she go to his house? The two places were in opposite directions. Time was running out. Judith was beginning to think Abe might have a point about telephones.

When Judith left home, her mother had been on her way up the stairs to the main bedroom. She intended to give birth to this baby in her own bed. Mama was calm and orderly, like she always was. The pot was on the stove for water to heat. Mama had even made a batch of bread that morning before the pains started. Then she left instructions for supper.

Had the baby already come? Judith wondered. Was she already too late finding Dr. Dan? She would keep looking, she decided, no matter how long it took. Despite her mother's organization, something could go wrong. Her mother might need a doctor.

"Judith! What are you doing here?"

Relief washed over her as Judith saw Dr. Dan come around the corner from the side of the clinic. His tall form cast a shadow over her spot on the wooden sidewalk. Judith scrambled to her feet.

"Is it your mother?" Dr. Dan asked.

Judith nodded. "The baby is on the way. Mama says the pains are coming fast."

"Then we should get moving, too," Dr. Dan said. He glanced at his watch. "Marcia is expecting me home for supper soon. I'll have to find a way to send a message."

"I could go," Judith offered half-heartedly.

Daniel smiled and shook his head. "No, I think you'd better come with me. You should be with your family when the baby comes. Besides, Marcia is used to my being late. She'll understand when I come home with some good news."

"I hope we can find a streetcar," Judith said weakly.

"Have you run all the way over here?" Dr. Dan asked.

Judith nodded. "I didn't think there was time to wait for a streetcar."

"You were probably right about that," Dr. Dan said. He raised his eyes toward the street. "But we are in luck. Here's a car going in our direction right now."

The horses pulling the wooden car slowed to a stop at the

nearest corner. Dr. Dan and Judith hurried over and hoisted themselves into the car. They sank side by side into a wooden seat toward the front as the car clattered and picked up speed again. Judith was grateful for the clip-clop of the horses' feet taking her home again. She slid forward in her seat and leaned out over the open side of the car, resting her arm on the ledge than ran along the length of the car. Judith groaned as the car once again slowed to let passengers get on and off at another corner. There would be many more corners before they got home. She wished that she and Dr. Dan were in their own carriage and could go directly to her house.

"Relax, Judith," Dr. Dan said, as if he were reading her thoughts. "We'll be there in just a few minutes."

"But Aunt Tina says Mama's babies always come fast."

"Alison and Tina know what they're doing," Dr. Dan said. With a slight pressure on her shoulder, he pulled Judith back in her seat.

Finally they reached the streetcar stop nearest her house. They jumped off the trolley and dashed the last two blocks to the Fisk house.

Polly met them at the door.

"Has the—?" Judith started to say.

Polly shook her head as she took Judith's coat. "Not yet. But Mama says it won't be much longer."

"I'll go right up," Dr. Dan said. He took the stairs two at a time.

Judith grabbed the banister at the bottom of the stairs and watched as Dr. Dan disappeared down the hallway at the top.

"I don't hear anything," Judith said.

"Don't worry, Judith, everything is going well," Polly said.

"Is my father upstairs?"

Polly nodded. "Your mother asked for him."

"And my brother?"

"Walter is outside. He was too nervous to stay in the house."

"I know how he feels." Judith looked up the stairs again.

"It will be so exciting to have a new baby around," Polly said, her eyes bright.

"We have Richard and Anna and Esther," Judith said. "Esther is still a baby."

"She's more than a year old," Polly observed. "I love babies. I hope your mother will let me take care of this baby. My mother is excited, too."

"I just want Mama to be all right."

"She will be."

Judith sat nervously in a stiff-backed dining room chair. Everyone was so excited about the new baby. What was wrong with things the way they were? she wondered.

"We brought the new afghan," Polly said, sitting across from Judith. "I think it's the prettiest one my mother has ever made. It's such a lovely shade of green."

Judith nodded absently. At the moment, she was not interested in the afghan. She just wanted to be sure her mother was all right.

"What was that?" Judith stiffened and whirled her head around to look up the stairs.

Polly laughed. "It sounded like a baby's cry to me."

"Are you sure?" Judith jumped up and lurched toward the stairs.

The cry came again, this time louder and more vigorous.

"That's a baby, all right," Polly said, grinning.

The crying stopped. Judith sat on the bottom step.

"What's happening?" she asked. "Why is it so quiet?"

The next sound they heard was footsteps coming down the hall. Judith sprang to her feet just as Aunt Tina appeared at the top of the stairs.

"Polly," Aunt Tina said, "you were right. It's a boy! Judith, come and meet your brother. His name is Theodore."

CHAPTER 3
Judith's Discovery

Abe Stevenson bounded down the boardwalk with his lanky eleven-year-old legs. For a Saturday afternoon in early December, the weather was pretty nice. The breeze gently brushed Abe's cheeks. The sun still glowed bright in the sky over Minneapolis, even though it was not as hot as it had been a few weeks ago.

Abe hoped Judith would be able to go with him to see the new Pillsbury mill. Ever since Teddy had been born a few weeks earlier, it seemed that Judith always had something she was supposed to be doing. She came to school tired and complained that she had been listening to Teddy cry all night.

At the Fisk house, Abe rapped sharply on the door with his knuckles.

"Come on in, Abe," his uncle Charles called.

Abe pushed the door open and stuck his head in. "How did you know it was me?"

"You're the only person I know who knocks on the door with that rhythm," Uncle Charles said, grinning from his armchair. He put down his newspaper and gestured that Abe should come in and sit down.

"I'll remember that next time and try something new," Abe said.

"Where are you and Judith off to today?"

"The new Pillsbury A mill," Abe said with enthusiasm.

"You've been down there before, haven't you?" Uncle Charles asked.

Abe nodded. "Yes, but it's still interesting. Imagine, the biggest, most productive flour mill in the whole United States is right here in Minneapolis."

"Do you think you will ever get tired of looking at it?"

Abe shook his head vigorously. "It's science in action. They have figured out how to make technology useful, and I could never get tired of that." Abe looked around. "Where is Judith?"

"She's helping her mother with the bed linens this morning. She will be down in a minute or two."

Judith's mother entered from the hallway, cradling her newborn son. "Well, if it isn't Mr. Adventure himself," she said. "Judith tells me you're off to see the mill again."

The proud father rose to his feet and stretched out his arms. "Let me take the baby," Uncle Charles said. "You should sit down and rest for a few minutes."

Aunt Alison surrendered the infant Theodore to her husband's arms. "I should go check and see how Judith is doing."

"Judith is fine. Sit down for a few minutes."

Abe smiled at his uncle's affectionate expression as he watched his wife sink wearily into the armchair. Uncle Charles began to pace gently with Teddy.

Abe craned his neck to get a look at his newest cousin, who slept peacefully in his father's arms.

"Judith says the baby cries a lot," Abe said.

His uncle nodded. "He has been a bit colicky. He doesn't rest well at night."

"And we have to hold him almost all the time during the day," Abe's aunt added.

"Can I see him?" Abe asked.

"Certainly." His uncle stopped pacing and gently tilted Theodore toward Abe. The tiny chest rose and fell in an even, rapid rhythm. The baby's little hands were tightened into fists and curled up close to his face.

"He's certainly sleeping well now," Abe said softly. He reached out and touched the soft brown hair on the top of Teddy's head. "He's not all red and wrinkled like he was when he was born."

"He's growing like a weed," his aunt said. "And I'm sure he'll outgrow the colic soon, too. Judith did."

"Judith had colic?" Abe asked.

His aunt nodded. "I was so jealous of your mother. You and Judith were born on the same day, but I'd get letters from your mother describing how you slept peacefully at night and smiled happily during the day. Meanwhile Judith screamed and twisted all day and night for weeks."

"I never knew that." Abe looked back at Teddy. "He's beautiful. It's hard to believe any of us were ever that tiny." Abe marveled at the tiny nose, the perfect miniature pink mouth.

"Ready to go?" Judith's voice came from the hall. Abe thought she sounded irritated. Perhaps she had had another night without enough sleep.

"Yep. I was just admiring your little brother." Abe's gaze was still fixed on his little cousin.

"Let's get going," Judith said. She went out the front door without even looking at the baby.

Abe excused himself as quickly as he could and followed her. He bounded down the front steps to the sidewalk. "Hey, what's going on?" Abe grabbed at Judith's elbow to make her slow down.

Judith pivoted on the sidewalk and clenched her fists. Her green eyes flared in indignation. "I can't believe you were doing that!"

"Doing what?"

"Cooing over Theodore like he's the only baby you've ever seen."

"He's only a few weeks old, and I've hardly seen him at all."

"You're just like the rest of them!" Judith spun around and started marching toward downtown.

Abe's long legs made it easy for him to keep up. "All I did was look at the baby while I waited for you."

"No one forced you to look at him."

"I don't understand what you are so mad about," Abe said. "He's just a baby. He can't have done anything to hurt you."

"My life was ruined when he was born."

"That's not his fault."

"Just never mind," Judith snapped. "But don't talk about Teddy."

"Fine. Have it your way. Are you sure you feel like doing this today?"

"There's nothing wrong with me that an afternoon out of the house won't cure."

For a long time, Abe didn't dare to speak. Judith would cool off if he just left her alone.

They came to the corner of Hennepin and Washington.

"Do you want to stop in Wagner's Store?" Abe offered. Usually Judith loved to go in that shop and smell the spices.

"No, thanks," Judith said. "I was just down here yesterday with my mother."

"What did you buy?"

"Cloth and thread. She wants me to cross-stitch a sampler."

"That sounds like a good project. What's it a picture of?"

"It's not a picture. It's a poem. I think it's a song, actually. My mother learned it from some Swedish friends."

"Is it a nice poem?"

Judith shrugged. "Mama thinks so. Something about God. I haven't really read it yet."

She pointed to a building across the street from the tea and spice store. "Is your father at the bank today?"

Abe shook his head. "My mother doesn't like it when he works on Saturdays, but he took home a whole stack of papers with numbers all over them."

"Why do you think he likes all those numbers?"

Abe shrugged. "I don't know. They're just squiggles on paper to me. It's not like it's electricity or something scientific. Just bank account numbers."

They walked down Hennepin Avenue toward the Mississippi River. Brick buildings, some of them ten stories high, surrounded them. Stores, offices, banks, and mill offices were everywhere in downtown Minneapolis. The business district known as Bridge Square was busy even on a Saturday. Perched on the west bank of the Mississippi, Bridge Square was the heart of downtown Minneapolis. Dress shops, drugstores, banks, the post office, and city hall all belonged to Bridge Square. The thriving district was wedged between Hennepin and Nicolett Avenues.

"Everything comes to life down here," Abe said. "When everything is boring at home and my father is counting numbers, I can come down here and imagine."

"Imagine what?" Judith asked.

"Imagine anything. The mills are the first place that anything new and exciting happens—like the way they figured out how to grind the hard spring wheat into as fine a flour as anyone could ask for."

"I can see the smoke from the mills," Judith said. Her spirits were starting to pick up.

Abe looked from left to right. Horse-drawn streetcars were lining up along Hennepin Avenue.

"Did I tell you that Mr. Pillsbury has an electric fan and a telephone in his office?" Abe asked brightly.

"Are you sure? An electric fan?"

Abe nodded vigorously. "He's always up-to-date with technology. He makes science work for him in his business. That's what I want to do."

"Run a flour mill?" Judith asked doubtfully.

"No! Make science work to really get things done."

"Maybe someday you'll invent something, if you don't blow up your lab first."

"Now you sound like my father. He doesn't believe I can do anything in my lab, either."

"I'm sorry," Judith said. "I didn't mean it that way. I'm sure you'll think of something really great some day."

"Right now I would settle for convincing my father to get a telephone."

Suddenly Abe threw out his left arm, smack into Judith's stomach. He pushed her back just as a streetcar whizzed by.

"Hey!" Judith protested.

"Sorry," Abe said, "but I didn't want you to get run over. There are so many streetcars down here that it gets hard to stay out of their way."

"Well, you didn't have to hit so hard."

They continued along Hennepin until they approached the river's edge. The only things between them and the mighty Mississippi were several sets of railroad tracks. Trains carried the flour from the mills to destinations all over the country. Beyond the trains were the St. Anthony Falls, the powerful surging waters that provided the energy for the mills. Tens of thousands of gallons of water tumbled over the falls every day. Yet the river continued on with an inexhaustible supply of water.

The wind sprayed them with the tiny droplets that were caught in the air as the river surged through town.

"Figuring out how to get power from the falls was the smartest thing anyone in this town has ever done," declared Abe. "That's what I mean by making science work for people."

A suspension bridge at the edge of Bridge Square connected the west side of Minneapolis with the city's eastern bank. Judith and Abe crossed the bridge to get a closer look at the Pillsbury A mill.

Seven stories high and a block wide, the great Pillsbury A flour mill towered over other buildings in the neighborhood. Only a few months old, the building still looked new and clean.

"Is it true that Pillsbury A is the biggest mill in the country?" Judith asked.

Abe nodded. "It produces more flour than any other mill. It has all the latest equipment. It would be too expensive for all the other mills to convert their machinery. That's one thing that my father is right about."

A train whistle made them step back, putting a safe distance between them and the tracks. The train rumbled past them, an enormous black engine and twelve cars ready to be loaded with flour destined for Chicago and Cleveland and even New York.

"My father says the railroad will go right across the river someday," Judith said. "Soon, he thinks."

"Your father is a railroad man, so I guess he would know," Abe said. "All we need are engineers to figure out how to build a bridge strong enough to support a train right through the falls."

"Papa says Jim Hill will be the person to do it," Judith said. "He wants his railroad to go all the way to the West Coast."

"I know," Abe said. "My father calls it 'Hill's Folly.' " He doesn't think it's possible. Other companies have tried, and they have all run out of money."

"What do you think?"

"I think anything is possible," Abe said confidently. "My father worries too much about what things will cost instead of what things can do."

"Somebody has to worry about what things cost," Judith observed.

"I suppose so," muttered Abe, "but why does it have to be my father? Just imagine what Minneapolis would be like with telephones and electric lights and electric streetcars. Jules Verne would never worry about what something would cost."

"Jules Verne is a writer. He thinks up stories of things that are not true. Your father is a banker. He has to think about what is true."

Abe sighed. Sometimes Judith was too practical—and too much like his father.

"But some of Jules Verne's stories could come true," Abe said, "if people just believed in them."

Judith flinched as something brushed against her leg. She looked down to see a honey gold kitten rubbing itself against her.

"Abe, look!" She stooped down and scooped up the kitten.

"It's just a cat," Abe said. "They're all over the place down here. The mills keep them to make sure the mice don't get out of control."

"He's just a kitten," Judith said. "Look how tiny he is. He can't be more than a couple months old." She lifted the kitten to her face and rubbed her cheek into its soft fur.

"His mother is probably looking for him," Abe said.

Judith looked around. Trains and streetcars and piles of brick were on every side of them. "How could he possibly find his mother now?"

"Animals have their ways, Judith. He'll be all right."

She shook her head. "No, I'm taking him home."

"What will your parents say?"

"I don't care what they say!" she said adamantly. "Besides, they probably won't even notice. The only thing they pay attention to these days is Theodore."

"Your mother is going to notice an animal in the house," warned Abe.

"I'll keep him out back. " She nuzzled the kitten, and the kitten purred softly. "I can make a warm place for him and bring him milk."

"He's going to get bigger and need more than milk. When it gets cold, he'll need someplace warm to sleep."

"I can take care of him. I want to keep him."

"Judith—"

"I've made up my mind. He's mine. His name is Clover because he looks like honey."

Chapter 4

Problems in the Lab

Four months later, Judith was still the proud owner of a growing kitten. She held Clover snugly with one arm and tugged at the wooden door of Abe's lab with the other. She almost lost her balance. She yanked on the door again. For a moment, she thought it was frozen shut. Finally it opened. Judith stuck her head in the small building, which was hardly more than a shed.

"Don't you think it's awfully cold to be out here?" she asked Abe.

"Close the door," he responded, without looking up.

"So you admit it's cold." Judith stepped inside the shed.

"No, I just asked you to close the door."

Judith did as Abe asked. "It's only the beginning of April. The

23

winter is hardly over, and you're out here half the day." Clover squirmed in her arms. Judith tightened her grip.

"This is my lab. This is where I work," Abe said matter-of-factly.

"You don't even have a sweater on."

"Sweaters are too bulky. They get in the way of my work." Abe still had not looked up at Judith.

In the corner of the lab, just inside the door, a barrel stood on end. Judith brushed some dirt off of it and sat down.

"Why don't you ever clean this place up?" she asked. She glanced around the lab. Spider webs hung from the corners, and the winter's dust was thick on the beakers and bottles strewn around the workbench.

"I like things just the way they are," Abe said. He turned to one side and flipped the pages of a book.

"What is all this stuff, anyway?"

"Just things I need for my work—my experiments. Unless you're a scientist, you wouldn't understand."

"Abe Stevenson, you're eleven years old. I'm exactly the same age as you are. In fact, I'm four hours older than you are. I can understand anything you can understand."

Abe shook his head. "But you're not a scientist."

"And you are?" Judith was doubtful.

"Thomas Edison was doing experiments with chemicals on a train when he was not much older than I am."

"So?"

"So he became an inventor when he grew up. I can't waste time cleaning a lab when I have things to do." Abe turned another page in the book.

Judith stroked the cat. "What's that book?"

"You're asking a lot of questions today."

"I'm interested."

"It's Jules Verne. *Twenty Thousand Leagues Under the Sea.*"

"What is it about?"

"The crew of a fantastic submarine is trying to find a sea monster. They find all sorts of spectacular stuff deep in the ocean."

"Do you really believe it's possible to do the things he talks about in his stories?"

"I believe you can't know what is possible until you try something."

Just then Clover squirmed out of Judith's arms. She felt him sliding away but could not stop him. The cat leaped up onto the workbench. He brushed up against a beaker of green liquid as his tail swept across the page of Abe's open book.

"Hey! What's that cat doing up here?"

"He won't hurt anything," Judith insisted. "He's just a kitten."

"He was a kitten when you found him. But that was almost four months ago. He's growing into a big cat."

"He's harmless," Judith insisted, reaching for the cat. He slithered out of her reach. His emerald eyes dared her to try again.

"Have you convinced your mother that he's harmless?" Abe challenged.

"She lets Clover sleep in my room now," Judith declared, "and she says Clover is the cleanest cat she's ever known."

"Well, keep him off of my workbench, just the same."

Judith made another grab for Clover and caught him. She held the cat close and tight, but she could not bring herself to scold him.

"How is your sampler coming?" Abe asked.

"I'm almost done with the border. It has blue and white flowers all around the edge, with green leaves."

"It sounds complicated."

"It is. It's taken me all winter to do the border."

"Are you ready to start the poem?"

"Soon."

"How does it go?"

"I can only remember the first verse:

25

Children of the heavenly Father,
  Safely in his bosom gather;
Nestling bird nor star in heaven,
  Such a refuge e'er was given."

"I like it," Abe said. He looked out the small square window over his workbench. He could see the back of his family's home. As chilly as the day was, his mother, his aunt, and his little cousin Theodore were enjoying the backyard. Bundled up from head to foot, Teddy was sitting on a blanket on the ground, flapping his arms in the air with a grin on his face.

"Teddy sure is cute," Abe said. "Look at that grin!"

Judith shrugged. "He's all right, as far as babies go."

"He's more than all right," Abe said. "He's one happy baby."

"He should be happy, considering all the attention he gets," Judith grumbled.

"All babies need attention." Abe turned back to his book.

"Not this much! First it was the colic. Then when he didn't have colic anymore, they were fussing over what to feed him. Now they act like he's the only baby in the world ever to sit up by himself."

Abe turned and looked at Judith. "Are you jealous of your baby brother?"

"You have no idea what it's like! Teddy this, Teddy that. You're lucky that your parents didn't have another baby. No one pays any attention to me at all. Even Walter is amused by Teddy and wants to take care of him."

"Why shouldn't Walter take care of Teddy? They're brothers."

"I, for one, get tired of taking care of Teddy all the time."

Abe decided to change the subject. "Is your whole family coming over for supper?"

Judith nodded. "Papa is supposed to meet us here later, after his shift at the railroad."

Abe smiled. "Good. I haven't seen him in awhile. I like your father."

"You have a father of your own, you know," Judith snapped. "You don't have to borrow mine all the time."

A shadow crossed Abe's face. "It's not the same." Abe never felt as comfortable with his own father as he did with Uncle Charles. Why couldn't Judith understand that?

Clover broke free again. In a flash, he jumped from Judith's lap to the workbench and started walking around.

"Get that cat off of here!" Abe shouted.

Judith sprang to her feet and reached for Clover. But the cat meowed and twisted out of her reach. He landed on Abe's wooden stool, then slithered to the floor and nuzzled his way into a shelf under the workbench.

Judith bent over and called him, but Clover ignored her. Just as Judith reached out to scoop him up, Clover leaped up and reversed his path. He sprang to the stool and then to the workbench. Before Judith could see what happened, she heard the tinkle of broken glass.

"Judith!"

"I'm sorry, Abe, I'm really sorry." Judith lurched for Clover, who sprang to the windowsill.

"You're too easy on him," Abe said. He reached out firmly and snatched Clover by the scruff of the neck. Looking at the cat, he said, "I ought to just throw you out the window." Clover's paws clawed the empty air.

Judith jumped forward. "Don't do that! He's my responsibility. I'll get you a new beaker or whatever that thing is." She grabbed her cat and held him close.

"I don't understand why you are so attached to that cat," Abe said, turning back to his bench. He started picking up the broken pieces of glass and piling them in one spot.

Judith buried her face in the cat's fur. "Clover needs me. He was a lost, hungry kitten when I found him. He needs me and he likes to have me around, even if no one else does."

"Don't you think you're exaggerating just a little bit?" Abe said. He wrapped the broken glass in an old newspaper. "It's not as if you're invisible or anything."

"You don't understand," Judith mumbled. "No one does."

"I do understand one thing," Abe said, picking up the bundle of newspaper. "I have to get rid of this broken glass. And leave that cat outside the next time you come."

He pushed open the door and went in search of a safe place to put the broken glass. Holding her cat, Judith watched him from across the yard. Once Abe had disposed of the glass, he turned his attention to Theodore.

Abe stretched himself out in the brittle spring grass and put his face level with Teddy's. He grinned into the bright blue eyes that greeted him. Immediately the infant tried to grab Abe's nose. Abe did not move fast enough.

"Ow!" Abe cried. "He's strong."

Judith thought Abe had gotten what he deserved. What did he expect when he stuck his face in front of a baby?

Mama laughed. "He likes to pull on everything, including noses."

"You were the same way, Abe," Aunt Tina said. "When you were a baby, you had to touch everything around you to see what it was made of and what it might do." She tilted her head thoughtfully to one side. "Come to think of it, you're still that way."

Abe smiled. "Maybe Teddy and I have more in common than I realized." He let Teddy grab at his nose again. Teddy gurgled in pleasure.

Abe scrambled to his feet. "I'd better get back to work."

"Supper will be ready in about thirty minutes," Abe's mother said. "Make sure you clean up in time to come to the table."

"Yes, Mama."

Judith waited for her cousin outside the little lab building, growing angrier as she watched.

"How could you do that?" she asked Abe as he approached.
"Do what?"

"I thought I could depend on you to see things from my point of view," Judith said, "but you're acting just like the rest of them. He's just a baby. Why does everyone act like he's something special?"

"He is something special," Abe said. "And I like having him around."

"You used to like having me around."

"I still do."

"You sound just like my father."

"Judith—"

But she was gone. All Abe could do was watch the back of her head as she stomped off toward the house with her cat.

CHAPTER 5
The Party

Judith watched as Abe threw himself forward and landed on his stomach. His outstretched arms missed their prey. As his chin scraped the dirt in his backyard, he sighed.

Annoyed, Judith plopped down on the back step of Abe's house. Sweat trickled down the back of her neck. The backyard was filling up for the late summer afternoon picnic lunch at the Stevenson house.

Teddy giggled and kept running. Even with the unsteady gait of a toddler, Teddy was in control and moving fast.

"Did he get away again?" Judith's father asked Abe.

Abe grinned and nodded.

Judith watched the cluster of adults that had gathered around her cousin. Mama and Papa glanced down at him before watching

Teddy toddle off. Dr. Dan and Aunt Marcia were nearby with their children Richard, Anna, and Esther.

"How can such a little child run so fast?" Abe asked. He stood up and dusted himself off. "He looks like he will tip over at any moment, but he just keeps going."

Mama smiled, too. "We were so surprised when he started walking. He was only nine months old! And he didn't waste any time learning to run."

Aunt Marcia took a step closer to Mama. She held her own youngest child in her arms. "Esther is a year older than Teddy, but I think he can outrun her already."

"I'm eleven years old—almost twelve," Abe said. "I should be able to catch him."

"He has a big head start on you now," Papa said. He pointed at Teddy, who was toddling past Abe's lab toward the far corner of the Stevensons' backyard.

Abe scrambled to his feet. "He shouldn't go in that part of the yard. He could get hurt." Once again, he was in pursuit of the drooling, giggling toddler.

Papa turned to Judith, who still sat on the steps and had not said a word. "Why don't you help Abe?"

"Help him do what?"

"Help him catch Teddy."

Judith shrugged. "He'll catch him. I think you're all exaggerating. Teddy isn't even a year old. He falls down every ten steps. He can't possibly outrun Abe."

"But it is fun to see him try," her father said, his proud eyes still fixed on his youngest child across the yard.

Judith rolled her eyes, but of course her father was looking at Teddy, so he didn't notice.

The back door of the Stevenson house opened, and Aunt Tina came out with a platter of summer fruit. Judith jumped up to get out of the way.

"Judith, can you help me with this?"

Judith reached out for the platter.

"Just set it on the table," her aunt Tina said, pointing to a wooden table covered with a checkered cloth.

The table was already covered with platters of bread, meats, garden vegetables, and sweets. Judith nudged a platter of ham a couple of inches to the left and made room for the fruit tray. They had far too much food, she concluded, even for three families. But that's the way her aunt Tina was, always making sure no one needed anything.

"I was hoping it would cool off a bit today." Aunt Tina wiped her forehead with the back of her hand. "Enoch is not fond of the heat."

"Where is the birthday boy?" Dr. Dan asked. "Let's get this celebration going."

"He promised to come out in just a few minutes," Aunt Tina said.

Papa wrinkled his forehead doubtfully. "He's not working on his birthday, is he?"

"I'm afraid so," Aunt Tina replied. "Something about financing a stretch of railroad."

"Jim Hill's railroad?"

"Hill's Folly, as Enoch calls it."

"He's wrong about that, you know," Papa said.

"Enoch has a very good reputation in these matters," Aunt Tina replied.

"He can't deny the progress of the railroad."

"Enoch is merely questioning whether there is an adequate financial base for the project."

Aunt Marcia jumped in. "Let's not talk about business."

Esther squirmed to get out of Aunt Marcia's arms and started toward the fruit on the edge of the table. Her tiny fingers gripped the edge of the table and she pushed herself up on her tiptoes.

"Judith—stop her," Aunt Marcia pleaded.

Judith was used to having a toddler around. She knew what to do. She scooped up her little cousin and stepped back from the table.

"It looks like Esther is ready to eat," Aunt Tina said, chuckling. "I'll go see what's keeping Enoch. Judith, why don't you round up the rest of the children?"

Judith surveyed the backyard. Abe had Teddy well under control now. But nobody had been paying any attention to Richard and Anna. The two of them had climbed a tree stump outside of Abe's lab and were leaning precariously toward the window. They wanted to see what was inside.

Judith handed Esther to her mother and started for the lab. Sneaking up from behind, she snatched three-year-old Anna off the tree stump. Anna squealed in protest. Richard, five years old, jumped in surprise. One at a time, Judith lifted them off the stump and set them on firm ground. Scowling at the two of them, Judith shook an index finger.

"You know you're supposed to stay away from the lab," she said.

"We didn't go in," Richard said in his own defense. "We just looked in the window."

"But you could get hurt climbing up here," Judith said.

"Why does Abe have a lab?" Richard asked.

"What's a lab?" Anna asked.

Judith sighed. How could she explain Abe's lab to these two when she did not really understand it herself?

"Abe likes to find out how things work," Judith finally said.

"Is that what he does in there?" Richard asked.

Judith nodded.

"Why does he need all those bottles?"

Judith shrugged. "The bottles are chemicals, I think."

"What are chemicals?" Esther asked.

Judith sighed again.

Behind her came a laugh. She turned to see Abe with Teddy squirming in his arms.

"Have they got you stumped?" Abe asked, his eyes twinkling.

"If you think it's so funny," Judith said, "you try explaining it to them." She glanced back at the house. "Your mama says it's almost time to eat."

"Eat! Eat!" Anna squealed and started running toward the house.

"Put Teddy down," Judith said.

"I'm about to lose my grip anyway," Abe said, setting the baby on the ground and pointing him toward the house. Teddy chased after Richard and Anna.

"Here comes your father," said Judith.

"Finally," Abe said. "I'm starving. Mama wouldn't let me eat a bite."

"He looks happy."

"Who?"

"Your father. He looks happy."

Abe squinted toward the back of the house. His father was smiling as the children gathered around him. He leaned down, and Anna gave him a dutiful birthday kiss. Teddy lost his balance and sat on his uncle Enoch's big black shoe. Everyone laughed.

"You're right," Abe agreed. "He was working all morning. I was sure he would be too busy to come out."

"He had to come," Judith reminded Abe. "It's his own birthday party."

"I'm sure he only came to please my mother."

"Don't be ridiculous. He's having a wonderful time." Judith watched as her uncle Enoch picked up Teddy and tossed him gently in the air. The little boy howled with delight as his uncle caught him again.

"I'll bet your father used to do that with you," Judith said.

Abe shrugged. "I don't remember. He doesn't talk to me very much now."

Judith glanced sideways at Abe. "I know what you mean." Her own father had Teddy now. "Do you remember our birthday last year?" Judith asked.

Abe nodded. "Right before Teddy was born. Everybody thought it would have been wonderful if the baby had been born on our birthday."

"I'm glad he wasn't. I don't mind sharing my birthday with you," Judith said. "But I would have hated it if Teddy had been born on our birthday."

"Come and eat!" Abe's mother called. Abe and Judith crossed the yard.

"Fill your plates at the table," Aunt Tina said, "then the children can sit on the quilts. Abe, Judith, be sure to help the little ones."

"What about Walter and Polly?" Judith asked.

"They're old enough to sit at the table with the adults," her aunt answered.

Judith looked at Abe with a distinct frown. "That's not fair," she muttered.

Eventually everyone had a plate of food. Richard, Esther, and Anna were settled on a quilt with Abe and Judith. Teddy roamed around, too young to eat the picnic fare.

Hungry, the children munched without talking much. Judith settled herself on the corner of the quilt nearest the adult table.

"It's amazing how Ted gets around," Aunt Tina said. All heads turned to watch the little boy carefully squat over a daisy and gently touch its petals.

"He loves to touch things," Papa said. "Most kids would tear that flower up, but not Theodore."

"You have a sensible boy there," Uncle Enoch said.

Judith rolled her eyes. Abe saw her and snickered.

"Having another child is one of the best things we've ever done," Mama said, taking Papa's hand. "Little Theodore is a bundle of surprises, and we're enjoying every one of them."

"In fact," Papa said, "we think it might be nice to have another baby. Walter and Judith had each other while they were growing up, but they are so much older than Teddy. He needs a playmate."

Judith dropped her fork on Richard's knee.

"Ow!"

Ignoring Richard, Judith hissed at Abe. "Did you hear what my father just said?"

Abe nodded. "I think he's right. It would be nice if Teddy had a brother or sister to grow up with."

"Teddy, Teddy, Teddy! Is that all anyone ever thinks about?" Judith picked up her fork and stabbed a meatball viciously.

"You hurt me!" Richard declared.

Just at that moment, Teddy tumbled into Abe's lap. Abe whisked his plate out of Ted's reach just in time. Judith stood up and casually walked over to where her parents were sitting.

"Papa, would you pass me the fruit, please?" she asked sweetly.

Papa held out the fruit tray as he glanced toward the quilt. "Is Teddy all right over there?"

"This is a wonderful meal, Aunt Tina," Judith said. She reached into a basket for a second biscuit.

Papa caught Judith's eye. "Why don't you feed Teddy a bit of banana? You know how much he loves them."

Judith looked at the banana she had put on her plate a few seconds ago. How could she refuse Papa's request? "Yes, Papa."

When Judith sat down again she bumped Richard's shoulder.

"Hey!"

"You can't tell me you didn't see that," Judith hissed at Abe as she broke off a piece of banana and offered it to her little brother. Teddy picked it up with his chubby fingers and continued roaming the yard as he stuffed it in his mouth.

"All he did was ask you to feed Teddy something."

"He didn't ask if I was all right," Judith said. "He didn't ask if I was getting enough to eat."

Abe shrugged. "He knows you're old enough to take care of yourself. Teddy's not. You have to understand your father's point of view."

"If you're such an expert on fathers, go talk to your own.

Maybe the reason he doesn't talk to you is that you don't talk to him! At least I tried."

Aunt Tina disappeared into the house and returned with a cake.

"Chocolate!" Richard squealed.

Dr. Dan held Richard back long enough for Uncle Enoch to get a good look at his cake. Then Richard insisted on having the first piece. Mama and Aunt Tina passed cake around to everyone.

Judith had barely started eating her piece when Uncle Enoch stood up.

"This has been delightful," he said. "And I hope you will all stay for a while longer. If you will excuse me, I must finish looking at some papers."

Although everyone protested his departure, Uncle Enoch started for the house. Judith noticed that Abe stiffened as he watched his father lean to the left, then drag his stiff right leg behind him.

CHAPTER 6

A Project Gets Ruined

"Do you think your father is right?"

Judith wrapped her arms around her knees and put her chin on them. She sat on a step below Abe's front porch.

"Right about what?" Abe responded. He sat next to Judith on the front step. Sun had overtaken the backyard. After lunch, everyone moved around seeking shade.

"The railroad. I heard your mother say he calls the railroad 'Hill's Folly.' "

"Lots of people call it that. He didn't make it up."

"But he does think it's a folly, doesn't he?"

"My father is very conservative," Abe said. "Building a railroad that goes all the way to the West Coast is risky. Jim Hill could lose a lot of money if it doesn't work."

"But it's Mr. Hill's money. Why does your father care?"

"Jim Hill is always looking for investors. He wants my father's bank to invest in the new railroad."

"Will they?"

Abe shook his head. "Not if my father has anything to say about it."

"He's pretty important at his bank, isn't he?" Judith said.

Abe nodded. He turned his head from left to right, scanning the yard. "Where's Teddy?"

"Napping," Judith answered. "So are Esther and Anna. Finally, we can have some peace and quiet."

"It's not so bad with all the little kids around," Abe said, "as long as they stay out of my lab."

"You can say that because you don't have any little kids living at your house," Judith observed. "They just come and visit and then go home. But Teddy is always around at my house."

Abe bent over and picked up a stick. It was thin and straight, with small nubs growing off one side.

"Look at this," he said. "It looks like part of a railroad track." Abe picked up another stick and held it right up against the first stick. They fit together perfectly.

"You're right," Judith said. "Hey, let's build a railroad around the yard."

"Great idea," Abe said. "I'm bored just sitting here anyway. Mama made me promise not to go in my lab while we have company."

They hopped off the porch and began scrounging for sticks and branches that looked like they could be transformed into railroad tracks. On the front porch steps, they laid the sticks out in neat piles. They sorted them by length.

"We need more little ones to be cross ties," Abe said. He let the dirt sift out of his hand so that only tiny twigs remained. "Like these!"

"Here's one that's curved!" Judith held up her prize stick.

"Good. Find some more like that. We'll circle the tracks around the maple tree."

They worked steadily after that, searching out sticks, matching them up, laying them end to end around the yard.

"I thought you didn't like railroads," Abe said to Judith as they searched for more bent sticks to go around the tree.

Judith shrugged. "I don't get as excited as you and Papa do, but I suppose they are a little bit interesting."

Abe grinned. "You'll come around."

"Well, maybe if I understand railroads a little bit better, my father will be more interested in me."

"Your father is interested in you," Abe said emphatically. "Why can't you see that?"

"Do you think your father is interested in you?" Judith challenged.

Abe did not answer. Judith turned her attention back to the project.

"We can make this look like a town," she said.

She stood several dried pine cones in clusters to create groves of trees.

"We need some bridges if this is going to be like Minneapolis," Abe said. He knelt in the dirt and began digging trenches with his fingers and built bridges over them.

Nearly two hours passed. Hardly any loose sticks were left in the yard. Every branch and twig had been put to use in the construction project.

The front door opened. Abe did not have to look up to see who was coming. He recognized the uneven step that he heard on the porch. His father had come outside. Abe focused on balancing a delicate twig across a bridge.

"Hello, Uncle Enoch," Judith said.

"What are the two of you up to, now?" he asked.

"We're building a railroad."

Uncle Enoch nodded silently, but he did not say anything.

"Do you like it?" Judith asked. "We've worked all afternoon on it."

"I can see that," Uncle Enoch said. "It's quite elaborate."

"Thank you." Judith was quite proud of their effort.

Abe started digging another trench, even though he did not have any more twigs for bridges.

"You know," Uncle Enoch said, "a railroad like that would be very expensive to build."

Judith shrugged. "We just used what we could find."

"It looks to me like you've just about run out of sticks."

"Then I guess we're finished," Judith said.

Uncle Enoch pointed to a corner of the yard. "But look over there. The track leads nowhere."

Judith looked where he pointed, puzzled. They had run out of sticks in that corner of the yard. But why was Uncle Enoch pointing that out?

Abe stopped digging and looked at his father. "Papa, you're trying to say that we've run out of money, aren't you?"

"I'm simply pointing out that perhaps you could have planned more carefully. Then you wouldn't have a track that leads nowhere."

Abe did not say anything, but he caught Judith's eye.

"I suppose you're right, Uncle Enoch," Judith said. "It was such fun building that I didn't think about what would happen when we ran out of sticks."

Uncle Enoch laughed gently. "You and Jim Hill."

"You don't think he's going to be able to build his railroad to the West Coast, do you?" Abe asked.

Uncle Enoch shook his head. "I'm not sure he'll make it across Minneapolis. He's a dreamer."

Abe caught Judith's eye again, then turned back to the dirt.

"What's wrong with dreaming?" Judith asked. She could say things to Uncle Enoch that Abe would not say. "Nothing new would ever happen if people didn't dream."

"Dreams cost money," Uncle Enoch said. "But the dreamers never think about that. When they run out of money, they come to the bank to ask for more. Bankers have to think about the bottom line."

"My father says that the railroads have made this country what it is today," Judith said.

"Ah, yes," Uncle Enoch answered, "but the banks made the railroads what they are today." He nodded toward Abe. "Abraham should be thinking about a career in banking. That's where the real future is."

"I'm not very good with numbers," Abe mumbled.

"Nonsense," his father said. "Anyone can learn to figure. I don't want to see you give your life to something like the railroad when you could do so much better for yourself."

"Yes, Papa," Abe said softly.

"But Abe doesn't want to work for the railroad," Judith said. She ignored the angry dart Abe threw at her with his eyes. "Abe wants to be an inventor. That's why he has a lab. That's why he studies science all the time."

Uncle Enoch shook his head. "Science costs money, too. In fact, it costs more than the railroads, I think. People spend years and years and thousands and thousands of dollars looking for new and better ways to do things when there is nothing wrong with the old ways."

"But maybe Abe will do something really wonderful," Judith persisted, "like inventing the telephone or discovering electricity."

The front door opened again, ending the debate—at least for the moment.

"Hi, Papa!" Judith greeted her own father.

"Hello, Judith. My goodness, Abe, what have you done out here?"

Abe brightened and scrambled up out of the dirt. "It's a railroad!"

"I can see that. It's quite impressive."

"It's got bridges and tunnels, and it goes through pine groves."

"It's a bit like Minneapolis, isn't it?"

Abe beamed while Judith's father came down off the porch to inspect the workmanship. He squatted over the bridge Abe had just finished. Judith stood to the side with her arms crossed across her chest. Her father had hardly spoken to her.

"Enoch, you should be proud of Abe," Papa said. "This is a work of art."

"I believe your daughter had something to do with it, too," Uncle Enoch said.

Papa turned to Judith. "Is that true?"

Judith nodded.

"Actually, it was her idea," Abe confessed. "She found the bent twigs to go around the tree."

Papa nodded his satisfaction. "I had no idea you were interested in the railroad."

Judith started to smile, ever so slightly. Her father had noticed her! "You and Abe talk about railroads all the time. I've learned a lot by listening."

"Is that so? I wonder what other secrets you're keeping." He smiled at Judith.

The gate to the side yard creaked. Mama pushed it open and let Teddy out into the front yard.

"Look who's up from his nap!" Papa said. He spread open his arms to welcome his small son.

Teddy charged forward and tumbled into his father's arms.

"We were just discussing the financing of railroads," Uncle Enoch said.

"That sounds like a banker," Papa said. Teddy squirmed in his arms. "Just let me have my tracks and engines and goods to move around the country."

"And that sounds like a railroad man," Uncle Enoch said, with the slightest of twinkles in his eye.

"I think we have a good arrangement," Papa said, "a banker

43

and a railroad man in the family. And, of course, Daniel is a doctor." He nodded his head toward Abe. "And before long, we'll have a scientist."

"Well, it's a bit early to be certain about that," Uncle Enoch said.

Abe dropped to the ground again and dug his fingers into the dirt. He did not really need another canal, but he could not keep his fingers still.

Teddy writhed in his father's arms.

"I guess this little guy wants down," Papa said. And he set Ted on the ground.

"No!" cried Judith as Teddy started running. He was headed straight for the maple tree. With one foot he tore up a bridge. Three steps later he crunched Judith's pine grove. Judith tried to catch him, but she only made things worse. She could not watch her brother and watch where she stepped at the same time. A snap under her left foot told her that she had stepped right into the longest canal Abe had dug. "Theodore!"

Teddy stopped suddenly, lost his balance, and sat awkwardly on the most detailed stretch of curved stick track. In a second, he was on his feet again with his fists full of twigs. Gleefully he threw them in the air, then turned and looked for his father's approval.

Judith stopped trying to catch her brother. "Oh, Teddy," she groaned. She dropped to the ground herself. In a second, Abe was at her side.

They surveyed the damage. The afternoon's work was in shambles. Anyone who had not seen the miniature wooden railroad would never guess it had been there. Teddy was now in his father's arms. Judith waited for Papa to scold Teddy, but he didn't say anything.

"He's moves fast, doesn't he?" Abe said.

"It's all wrecked."

"We could rebuild."

Judith shook her head. "No. There's no point. The wind would blow it all away overnight, anyway."

Uncle Enoch chuckled from the porch. "You're right about that, Judith. That's what happens to real railroads, too."

CHAPTER 7
Abe's Experiment

"I'm glad you didn't bring your cat," Abe said a few weeks later as he tightened a copper coil at the base of a glass bulb and squinted to inspect his work. He pressed his lips together in concentration.

"I couldn't wake Clover up," Judith said, chuckling softly. "'Mama says Clover has turned into a lazy good-for-nothing. He won't even chase the mice in our basement anymore, and he hasn't caught a bird since the spring."

"You should never have taken him away from the mill," remarked Abe.

"He was a hungry little kitten. I couldn't leave him there."

"He would have learned to look after himself. He's gotten used to you feeding him. Why should he bother with birds and mice?"

"I don't care." Judith tossed her head in defiance. "Teddy

can't look after himself, either, but we keep him around."

Abe scrunched up his face. "How can you compare your little brother to a stray cat?"

Judith shrugged. "Teddy is okay, I suppose, but he's more work than Clover—a lot more."

"Neither of them belongs in my lab." Abe attached the other end of the coil to a box with a crank.

"At least it's not as hot out here as it was on your father's birthday," Judith said. She sat on her usual upturned barrel in the corner of the lab.

"In the winter you said it was too cold. In the summer, it was too hot. Make up your mind."

"I have made up my mind," Judith retorted. "I like the early fall—like it is right now."

"The temperature makes no difference to me. Thomas Edison would never have invented the lightbulb if he'd worried about things like that."

"The only problem with the fall is that it gets dark earlier," Judith said. "How can you see what you're doing?"

"I'm trying to fix that problem."

Judith inspected Abe's contraption. "Is that really going to work?"

"One more coil," Abe said as he broke off just the length he needed.

"Is that glass tube supposed to light up?"

"I hope so. I just have to generate enough energy with the crank."

Judith laughed. "You should get Teddy to come over here and turn it. He has lots of energy."

Abe raised an eyebrow. "The challenge would be to control his energy to make it do what we want it to do."

Judith laughed again. "We would all be a lot less tired if we knew how to do that."

"What I mean," Abe continued, "is that there are many forms

of energy in the world. Jules Verne writes about them all the time. For instance, take the St. Anthony Falls. It's hard to even count the number of gallons of water that go over the falls every day. And the water is so powerful it could kill you if you tried to ride a boat over the falls."

"I would never try that!"

"There has to be a way to put that power to use."

"The mills are already using water power," Judith said. "That's why Pillsbury built right in that spot."

Abe shook his head. "No, I'm talking about electricity. There has to be a way to generate electricity from the waterfalls." He checked his last coil. "There. We're ready to go."

"Can I try?" Judith asked.

Abe hesitated. "You have to crank really hard."

"I'm as strong as you are," Judith asserted.

Abe moved out of the way, and Judith stepped over to the box with the crank.

"Lean on it," Abe instructed, "so you can put all your strength into the crank."

Judith bit her bottom lip and followed his instructions. She began to turn the crank. She could not help looking at the glass tube. Nothing was happening.

"Harder," Abe urged. "Faster."

Judith cranked harder and faster. Still nothing happened.

"Here, let me try." Abe nudged Judith out of the way and took over the crank. He gripped the handle and spun the crank faster than Judith could have. But the glass tube did not light up.

The door to the lab opened.

"What's going on in here?" Papa said, smiling at Abe and Judith.

Papa must have come straight from work, Judith thought. His face was slightly grimy.

"Is there a secret experiment in progress?" Papa asked.

Abe sank onto the barrel. "No," he muttered. "It's not working."

"Can I help?" Papa asked.

Abe shook his head. "No, thank you, Uncle Charles. I have to figure this out for myself."

"Oh, come on, Abe," Papa persisted. "Surely Thomas Edison and Alexander Graham Bell have assistants."

Abe sighed. "I must not have the coils right. I'll have to start over."

"Is it time to go home for supper, Papa?" Judith asked.

Papa shook his head. "No, I just came out to talk to Abe for a bit. Hey, Abe, maybe a baseball game would cheer you up."

"A ball game?" Abe perked up.

Papa nodded. "Tomorrow afternoon. It's Saturday. No work, no school. What do you say?"

"I'd love to! What time?"

"I'll come by for you about eleven o'clock."

"Perfect!"

"What about me?" Judith asked softly.

Papa and Abe turned to look at her. Papa raised en eyebrow, questioning.

"I like to go to baseball games, too."

"Oh, certainly," Papa said. "You shall come if you want to."

"I do want to."

Papa turned back to the workbench. "Why don't we have another go with these coils right now?"

"Are you sure you have time?" Abe asked.

"Of course."

Judith inched back toward the door. Papa and Abe bent their matching brown heads over the glass tube.

Judith stepped outside the door. How could her own father invite Abe to a baseball game with Judith standing right there? How could he do that and not invite her, too?

She slammed the wooden door and marched across the yard.

Inside the lab, Judith's father and Abe looked at each other.

"What's wrong with Judith?" Judith's father asked.

Abe pushed a small box toward the back of the workbench. He shrugged but did not say anything.

"Abe?"

"Yes, Uncle Charles?"

"You do know what is bothering Judith, don't you?"

"She'll be all right."

"But something is wrong, isn't it? Ever since Theodore was born, Judith has acted strangely. He's almost a year old now. I was hoping she would be used to having him in the family."

Abe fidgeted with the handle of a hammer.

"Am I right, Abe?"

Abe nodded slightly. "I think you should ask Judith these questions."

Judith's father sighed. "Yes, you're right."

Judith opened the back door to Abe's house and went in search of her mother and little brother. At that moment, she thought she would be happier to be with Teddy than with her father. But the house sounded empty.

"Mama?" she called.

No one was in the kitchen. Judith moved through the dining room and down the hall. "Mama? Aunt Tina?"

Uncle Enoch appeared from his study. "Hello, Judith."

"Hello, Uncle Enoch. I thought you would still be at the bank."

"There is far too much commotion down there today," Uncle Enoch said. "I have some important papers to review, and I thought it would be quieter here."

Judith looked around. It was quiet. But it should have been noisy. Where was everybody?

"Where is my mama?" she asked.

"She and Aunt Tina have gone out shopping. They went down to the dress shop on Washington Avenue."

"I like that shop," Judith said with disappointment.

Uncle Enoch shrugged. "They probably did not know that you wanted to go."

"Did they take Teddy?"

"Yes, of course. I'm afraid I'm not much of a nursemaid."

Judith sighed. She would have to go back out to the lab with her father or sit in the house with her uncle. She did not want to do either one.

"Is Abraham still out in the lab?" Uncle Enoch asked.

Judith nodded. "His experiment didn't work. Papa is trying to help him."

"I'm afraid your father fills Abraham's head with big ideas."

Judith straightened up. "This experiment is important to Abe. Science is important to Abe."

Uncle Enoch looked a bit shocked that Judith had spoken as she had.

"I'm sorry, Uncle Enoch. I don't mean to be disrespectful."

"No, I don't suppose you do. You understand, of course, that I want what is best for Abe."

Judith nodded. "I know that."

"Abe can be a difficult boy, Judith." Uncle Enoch took off his glasses and folded them into his shirt pocket. "He means no harm, I am sure. But he sometimes insists on his own way even when it is not logical."

"Yes, sir, Uncle Enoch." Judith did not know what else to say.

"As his father, it is my job to provide guidance, even when he does not see the reasons. Even if he's going to be a scientist, he has to have his feet firmly on the ground. Life is not a Jules Verne novel."

"Yes, sir."

Uncle Enoch's expression softened. "I'm sorry that you missed the shopping expedition."

"It's all right. I don't need any new dresses anyway."

"That's quite a sensible thing to say," Uncle Enoch said

approvingly. "If you'll excuse me, I have just a bit more work to finish up."

Judith nodded. "Good-bye, Uncle Enoch."

Uncle Enoch closed the door to his study and left Judith standing in the hall. She felt odd. She was virtually alone in a house that was not hers. What was she going to do now?

Judith remembered her sampler, stuffed into a bag that her mother always carried with her quilting projects. In the kitchen, the bag was in plain sight on the table. Judith fished out her sampler and smoothed it out. She had not worked on it very much since the start of the new school year. In shades of blue and red, the words to the song danced on the fabric:

Children of the heavenly Father,
  Safely in His bosom gather,
Nestling bird nor star in heaven
  Such a refuge e'er was given.

God His own doth tend and nourish,
  In His holy courts they flourish;
From all evil things He spares them,
  In His mighty arms He bears them.

Is that what Uncle Enoch was talking about? Judith wondered. Was he trying to spare Abe from some trouble?

She knew she'd sounded disrespectful when she'd challenged Uncle Enoch. But Abe had given up talking to his father. If Abe was going to borrow her father all the time, Judith at least wanted to understand why. Uncle Enoch seemed harsh sometimes, but she was sure he really cared about Abe.

The back door opened, and Papa came in.

"Judith, I'm glad I found you. I'm going to take the streetcar downtown and meet your mother. Do you want to come?"

A streetcar ride alone with her father? Judith could not believe what she was hearing. She nodded her head vigorously.

"I would love to go downtown."

"We'll have to hurry," her father said. "The shop will close soon."

"I just want to run out and say good-bye to Abe."

"Come right back."

Judith dashed across the yard and yanked open the lab door.

"My father asked me to take a streetcar ride," she said breathlessly.

Abe smiled. "That's good!"

"Your father is trying to help you, you know," Judith said.

Abe blinked at her. "What did the two of you talk about?"

"Oh, different things."

"Your father understands you, too," Abe said.

"And what did the two of you talk about?" Judith countered.

Abe smiled slightly. "Different things."

"I just came to say good-bye."

Judith closed the lab door gently this time.

CHAPTER 8
Left Out

"These are great seats!" Abe fell into a clattering wooden chair behind first base, only three rows up from the playing field. The sun was strong but not overpowering. Green, lush grass rolled out over the field. Clean white base bags marked out the diamond.

Judith tumbled into the seat next to Abe. "Will it be a good game?" she asked.

"The teams are evenly matched," Papa answered as he sat on the other side of Judith. "The winning team will be the one with the best hurling."

"Were you a good hurler when you were young?" Abe asked.

"Oh, I was about average," Papa answered. "The baseball star in our family was your uncle David."

"Mama says Aunt Daria wasn't too bad, either," Abe said.

Papa chuckled. "She was feisty, that's for sure. She wasn't about to let David be better at anything than she was."

"Why should she?" Judith spoke up.

Papa laughed louder. "You are a lot like Daria. Having the two of you around is like—"

"We know," Judith said, "it's like having twins in the family all over again." She turned her eyes to the field. "How much longer before the game starts?"

Papa checked his watch. "Forty minutes."

"Good," Judith said. "We have plenty of time to get some peanuts."

"What's a baseball game without peanuts?" Papa asked as he reached into his pocket. He handed Judith a few coins. "Why don't you go get us three bags?"

"I saw a vendor right outside the front gate," Abe said, pointing in the direction from which they had come.

Judith waited for Abe to volunteer to go with her. He didn't. Papa and Abe both leaned back comfortably in their seats to watch the players warm up.

In the long line at the peanut stand, Judith stood squinting into the sun. People were still coming into the park in droves. Papa had said there might be six thousand people in the park by the time the game started. Judith tried hard to imagine six thousand people in one place.

The line inched forward. Behind Judith rose the wooden stands, rows and rows of seats filling steadily with ardent baseball fans. Judith wondered how the men could stand to wear dark suits and hats on such a warm day. Around the house, Papa always took his jacket off. But at the baseball park, he would keep it on, just like all the other men. Soon Abe would be old enough that he would have to wear a suit and hat.

Only three more people were ahead of Judith in the peanut line now.

At least some of the women in the stands allowed themselves the shade of a parasol. Judith wished she had thought to bring one. The sun was not hot, but it was bright. She should at least have worn a bonnet to shade her face.

Judith had not been to the baseball park very much. Papa used to go with her brother Walter nearly every weekend in the summer. Now sixteen years old, Walter was always busy with something or other. So Papa had started asking Abe. Judith had invited herself on this outing. Papa could hardly tell her she could not come after she said she wanted to. And Judith was not going to admit that she thought baseball was a slow, boring game. At least Papa had not tried to bring Teddy along. Even Papa knew that bringing a baby to a ballpark was asking for trouble.

Papa had acted strangely on the streetcar yesterday, Judith thought. He talked about dresses and hats and quilt patterns. Judith did not believe he was interested in any of those things. But he probably thought she was, so she had politely answered his questions. It was a strained conversation, not at all like the way Papa and Abe talked to each other. Judith was almost relieved when they got off the streetcar in front of the dress shop and Papa swooped Teddy up into his arms.

Her turn in line finally came. Judith paid for three bags of peanuts and started the climb back up to her seat.

Papa had moved over and taken Judith's seat, the one next to Abe. *I want to sit there,* Judith thought. But she could not very well make her father move. With a sigh, she sat in the seat Papa had left empty. Judith held out a bag of peanuts. Her father took it absently.

"Unions," Papa said.

"Unions?" Judith echoed. "Is there going to be a strike?"

"White Shirts," Abe said.

"Red Caps," Papa responded.

Judith was beginning to wonder if her father and cousin were speaking a secret code. If they did not want her to come to the ball-park with them, they should have said so yesterday.

"Saxons," Papa said.

"Ummm." Abe was stumped. "I know I'm forgetting something important."

"I'll give you a clue," Papa said. "You put it on your feet."

"Stockings?" Abe guessed.

"Yes, but what color?"

Judith looked at her stockings. Hers were brown. So she said, "Brown stockings?"

Papa looked at her in surprise. "I didn't know you knew that."

"Knew what?" Judith still did not know what she had said.

"Red?" Abe said.

Papa turned to Abe. "Yes, Red Stockings. And?"

Abe thought some more. "Blue," he said. "There were Blue Stockings, Red Stockings, and Brown Stockings."

"What are you talking about?" Judith pleaded. She opened her bag of peanuts, broke a shell, and tossed two nuts into her mouth.

"Teams," answered Abe. "Baseball teams of the Twin Cities."

"Let's not forget the North Stars," Papa said.

"And the Blue Stars," Abe countered.

"What about Gold Stars, Silver Stars, and Bronze Stars?" Judith asked.

Abe scowled. "Don't try to talk about things you don't know about. There are no such teams and never have been."

"Actually," Papa said, "Judith is right about the Silver Stars. There was a team with that name."

Judith smiled at Abe smugly. He ignored her.

"Have we named them all?" Abe asked.

"Well, let's see." Papa looked up at the blue sky, thinking. "Shirts Caps. . .I know one we missed—the Olympics."

"Most of those teams don't even play anymore," Judith observed. "How do you keep all that stuff straight in your brains?"

"It's easy to remember important stuff," Abe said airily.

Judith rolled her eyes, then repeated an earlier question. "How much longer until the game starts?"

The playing field was empty. After warming up, the players had returned to their dugouts.

"It should start any minute now," Papa assured Judith.

57

Within seconds the players from both teams poured onto the field. The cheering fans surged to their feet in the stands. Judith did as everyone else did: she stood and applauded. She was determined to pay attention and follow every play of this game. So what if she did not know the names of all the teams in Minneapolis and St. Paul? She knew the rules of baseball; she would be able to discuss this game intelligently.

When she sat down again, Judith found herself behind a large lavender parasol. Suddenly she did not think that parasols at the ballpark were such a good idea. With its ruffled trim, this one definitely belonged on a stroll through Bridge Square. Judith squirmed in her seat and craned her neck. It was no use. If she stayed in her seat, she would not see a thing. And if she could not see the game, she would never be able to discuss it intelligently with Papa.

"Papa, I can't see," Judith said bluntly.

"So far you have only missed the first pitch," Papa said, keeping his eyes on the field. "It was a ball."

"I don't want to miss any more." Judith stared at the top of the lavender parasol, wishing it to disappear. It twirled a couple times, but it was still there.

"I can't see!" Judith hissed.

"We might have to move to other seats." Papa did not turn to look at her.

"Did you see that?" exploded Abe. "What a pitch!"

Papa glanced around. "I don't see a place where we can all move," he said to Judith. "Do you want to sit on my lap?"

Judith scrunched up her face. "Papa! I'm almost twelve years old. I'm far too old for that."

The parasol twirled again, this time in the opposite direction.

"You could always look for another seat by yourself," Abe suggested. "There's an empty seat four rows behind us."

"Wow! That's a swing with snap," Papa said. He had lost interest in Judith's problem.

She craned her neck again, struggling to see around, above, or under the spinning parasol. *I always did think lavender was an ugly color,* she thought.

"Strike two!" called Abe.

Judith slumped back in her chair and crossed her arms across her chest. How could Papa and Abe even suggest that she go sit somewhere else, alone. Clearly neither of them planned to give up a spectacular seat only three rows behind first base. If she were a real baseball fan, she knew, she would go sit where she could see. It would not matter if she had to sit alone.

But it did matter. Judith glanced sideways at her father. He was leaning toward Abe, talking and pointing at something. In response, Abe grinned broadly. His brown eyes twinkled with the pleasure of being at the ball game with his uncle. Judith had hoped to feel that way on the streetcar the day before. Instead, she felt how hard her father strained to talk to her.

Crack! Suddenly the crowd rose to its feet. Judith followed suit. Even without seeing the pitch, she recognized the sound of wood meeting leather. It was a good solid hit to right field.

"Throw him out!" Abe screamed as the right fielder scooped up the ball on its first bounce and heaved it toward first base.

The runner beat the throw easily and was safe on first base.

Papa cupped his hands around his mouth. "We'll get the next one."

Papa nudged Abe with his elbow and said, "This is going to be an exciting game. I can feel it in my bones."

"One of the best!"

"Papa," Judith said as they all sat down again. "Was Uncle David really, really good at baseball?"

Papa nodded. "He spent a lot of time playing when he was about your age. All the hard work paid off. He was very good when he was in high school."

"I remember when he came to visit us from Cincinnati two years ago," Abe said. He kept his eyes on the field while he spoke.

"His windup was spectacular. I had to ask him not to hurl so fast."

Papa chuckled. "It was always that way when he was young. He's quite a good striker, too."

"Did he ever think about playing on a professional team?" Abe asked. "After all, the Cincinnati Reds were the first professional team, and he was right there in Cincinnati."

Papa nodded. "He dreamed of it, especially after the Reds got started. But right before the tryouts, he injured his leg and couldn't play. He never had another chance. He had to settle for being in the stands for the very first game."

"That's too bad," Judith said. Even though baseball was not her favorite activity, it saddened her to think that Uncle David had been cheated of his dream.

"How about you?" Papa turned to Abe. "Have you thought about playing ball?"

"Me?"

"Sure, why not? With some practice, you could be pretty good. It might be good for you to get out of that lab of yours a little more often."

"If I said I wanted to be a ballplayer, my father's heart would surely fail."

Papa sighed and shook his head. "I suppose that's true."

"I'm sure it's true," Abe insisted. "I can't even talk to him about being a scientist. He would throw me out of the house if I brought up baseball."

"Your father would never throw you out," Judith said, remembering Uncle Enoch's solemn expression the day before when he talked about his responsibility to guide Abe. "He only thinks about what's good for you. I think you should listen to him a little more often."

For the first time since the game began, Abe took his eyes off the playing field. He leaned forward, looked past his uncle, and stared at his cousin. Judith continued.

"Your father knows you have talents. He just wants you to use them well."

"I'll have to agree with Judith," Papa said. "I know your father cares for you, even if he does things in a different way than you expect."

Abe looked at his uncle, then back to Judith. His brown eyes captured her green ones. "I suppose all fathers are that way."

Judith looked away. The roar of the crowd responding to a hit saved her from having to answer.

CHAPTER 9
The First Lights

"Come on, Judith. Don't be so slow."

Abe marched three steps ahead of his cousin.

"I don't see why we have to be in such a hurry," Judith panted. It was the first time they'd gotten together since the ball game, and she wasn't sure she was happy to be spending time with her cousin.

"It will be crowded downtown. I want to find a spot where I can see what's going on."

Abe glanced over his shoulder. Judith was keeping up with him better than anyone else. His parents were a long way behind him. His father's war injury made it hard for him to walk very fast. Always patient, his mother walked steadily beside her husband.

They were enjoying the September evening stroll without worrying about finding a good spot.

"Don't you think we should wait for the others?" Judith asked. "I can't even see my parents anymore." In fact, she had not seen them for at least six blocks—ever since Abe had broken into a near trot headed for downtown.

"Don't worry about them," Abe replied as he continued on. "They'll look for us on Washington Avenue."

"You said there's going to be a big crowd," Judith said. She finally fell into step beside Abe. "They will never find us in a crowd."

"This is too important to miss," Abe insisted. "You can wait for them if you want to, but I'm going ahead."

Judith glanced back. Even now the crowd was growing so much that it would be hard to find her parents.

"I'll stay with you," she decided and quickened her pace. Being with Abe was better than being lost in the crowd alone.

They raced along Hennepin Avenue. Hundreds of other people had the same idea that Abe had. Along with everyone else, he was determined to witness the first electric lights in Minneapolis. This was the day that the Minnesota Brush Electric Company was going to show off their success. They were using the power of the St. Anthony Falls to generate electricity. And on this September evening in 1882, the first downtown lights would go on.

Abe and Judith turned down Washington Avenue and walked along the new cedar-block pavement.

"My father didn't even want to come," Abe said. "Mama convinced him the fresh air would do him good because he has been working so hard."

"My father couldn't wait to come," Judith said. "He's already thinking about what electricity could do for the railroad."

"Your father is a progressive thinker. My father is always suspicious of new ideas."

"Your father is a really good banker, a sensible man."

63

"What do you know about banking?" Abe asked doubtfully.

"I know that a lot of people respect your father. They must have good reasons."

"I suppose," Abe muttered, unconvinced.

Now they were in the block where the Big Boston Clothing Store was. People mixed around, chatting excitedly about what they were about to witness.

"Look at the water," Abe marveled. "It's still there. Using the falls to make electricity doesn't take away a single drop."

"You were right about this," Judith admitted. "You knew there had to be a way to do this."

Abe grinned. "Yep. And so much more is possible. I just know it."

They pushed their way through the crowd until they were right in front of the clothing store.

"There is where I want to stand," Abe declared. "Right here."

"Good," Judith smiled. "I love this store." She peered into the store window.

Abe laughed. "Your father says you love it too much. He's not sure he can afford to keep you around."

"He said that?" Judith was shocked. "He doesn't want me around?"

"He was just teasing! Can't you take a joke?"

"How can I be sure it's a joke?"

"Of course it's a joke. Don't be so sensitive."

"You wouldn't laugh if your father said something like that about you."

Abe had no answer. He wasn't sure his father would notice if he disappeared. Instead he said, "We'd better start looking for our folks."

Judith turned her attention back to the store window. "There's a new dress here that I really like. But it's getting too dark to see it."

"Just wait a few minutes," Abe said. "That's why we're here."

"Hello there!"

Judith spun around to see Dr. Dan standing behind her. Aunt Marcia was beside him, with Esther squirming in her arms. Richard and Anna chased each other around their mother's wool skirt.

"Where is everyone else?" Aunt Marcia asked.

Judith shrugged her shoulders. "They're coming. Abe was in a hurry."

"Richard is pretty excited, too," Dr. Dan said.

"Does he understand what is going to happen?"

"I explained everything to Richard," Abe informed Judith.

"So that a five-year-old can understand?" Judith challenged.

"He's a smart five-year-old," Abe answered.

"So now he knows all about hydroelectric power?" Judith looked at little Richard, who seemed more interested in the store window than anything else. "Perhaps I'll ask him to explain it to me."

"How is your cross-stitch project coming?" Aunt Marcia asked.

Judith frowned. "I'm not getting the lettering straight. I guess I'm not counting right. I've had to take the stitches out so many times that I've got the words memorized."

"What verse are you on?"

"I'm almost finished with the second one," Judith answered. And she quoted it:

> *"God his own doth tend and nourish,*
> *In His holy courts they flourish,*
> *From all evil things He spares them,*
> *In His mighty arms He bears them."*

"That's my favorite verse, I think," Aunt Marcia said. "Can you just imagine being in the arms of the heavenly Father?"

Judith smiled. "You say every verse is your favorite."

"I'd like to see it sometime."

"See what?" Mama and Papa had arrived. Teddy squealed at the sight of Abe.

"Judith's sampler," Aunt Marcia answered Mama.

"It's coming along nicely," Mama said. "Isn't that right, Charles?"

Papa pressed his eyebrows together. "Judith's sampler? I don't think I've seen it for quite some time."

More than a month, Judith thought. *You probably don't remember what it says.*

Teddy writhed in Mama's arms until she surrendered him to Papa.

"He's a wriggly little boy tonight," Papa said. He kissed Teddy's forehead. In response, Teddy arched his back and squawked.

"It's past his bedtime," Mama said. "I should have stayed home with him."

"No," said Abe. "This is going to be an historic event, Aunt Alison. You can't miss it."

"But Teddy is so tired."

"I'll take him," Abe volunteered. "I can make him happy."

Abe swung the toddler up on his shoulders. Teddy squealed in delight and drooled on top of Abe's head.

"Yuck," Judith said, scowling.

"Abe, here come your parents," Papa said.

Mama and Papa and Dr. Daniel and Aunt Marcia lifted their hands high. Aunt Tina and Uncle Enoch shuffled through the crowd toward them.

"I can hardly believe we all found each other," Aunt Tina said, "especially in the dark."

"What about Polly and Walter?" Aunt Marcia asked.

"They're off with their friends tonight," Mama explained.

Uncle Enoch scanned the crowd. "I'm surprised this many people would be so interested."

"Hey! Don't pull my hair!" Abe swiftly lowered Teddy to the ground. "Sorry, little guy. You can't do that."

Eleven-month-old Theodore Fisk dropped to the ground and squalled. With a sigh, Mama scooped him up out of the dirt.

Suddenly every face in the crowd was bathed in light. Teddy stopped bawling and held still. For half a minute or so, the whole crowd was hushed. Then the expressions of delight began.

"Wow!" Abe exclaimed. "They really did it—right on schedule."

"You sound surprised," Aunt Tina said.

"I'm amazed," Abe said, "not that they turned the lights on, but that somebody actually figured out how to do this."

"This will make shopping an entirely different experience."

The store window Judith had admired earlier featured a dark green suit with white trim. In the corner were a matching pair of boots all laced up. Judith was sure the suit would be perfect to highlight her own green eyes.

"Now look who's drooling," Abe teased.

"Don't be silly," Judith retorted. "I'm just looking in the window like I always do."

Beside Judith, two-year-old Esther pounded the glass. "Pretty dress."

"Yes, I like the dress," Judith said to Esther.

"Look across the street," said Dr. Dan.

Judith turned and looked. More lights illumined several businesses.

"It's like broad daylight," Mama said. "This was worth keeping Teddy up."

"Where is Teddy?" Papa asked.

Panic crossed Mama's face. "I thought you had him."

"He wanted down. I thought he went back to you."

"Teddy! Teddy!" Mama called through the crowd. "Come back to Mama."

"Abe!" Papa called. "Is Teddy with you?"

"Not since he pulled my hair." Abe pointed to a spot in front of the clothing store. "He was right there the last time I saw him."

"Well, he's not there now," Papa said. "Judith, Daniel, help us look for Ted. Alison, you stay right here in case he comes back."

Papa, Judith, Abe, Dr. Dan, and Uncle Enoch fanned out through the crowd, calling Teddy's name. Judith kept her eyes low to the ground, which made her bump into a few people. But Teddy was small, and he moved quickly.

"Thank goodness for these lights," Papa said. "It would be almost impossible to find him in this crowd in the dark."

It might be impossible anyway, Judith thought. But she said nothing. She just kept looking.

"Teddy! Teddy!"

At last came the cry, "Here he is."

Uncle Enoch had found the stray toddler down the block from the clothing store. Teddy was standing in front of a saloon, pointing at the lights above the doorway.

"Li, li," he said.

Papa scooped up Teddy just as Abe and Judith reached him. "Did you hear that?" Papa said excitedly. "He's saying 'light.' It's his first word."

Judith's stomach sank. Perfect little Teddy had frightened everyone half to death by running off. Now instead of being scolded, Teddy was getting his father's praise for saying his first word.

"Charles," Uncle Enoch said, "aren't you at all disturbed that you found your infant son standing in front of a saloon?"

"Teddy doesn't know what a saloon is," Papa answered. "He's not going inside for a glass of whiskey. He just likes the light."

Uncle Enoch scowled. "You know I don't approve of electrifying the downtown businesses. The fact that several saloons are among the first buildings to be electrified should tell you what a dangerous thing it is."

"The lights are not evil, Enoch," Papa said. "Whatever you think of the saloons, the lights helped us find Teddy."

"The same lights that attracted your son will attract other people to this place—people who will not have the good sense to turn around and walk away. Mark my words!"

"You're overreacting, Enoch."

Uncle Enoch shook his head as they all started walking back to the clothing store. His cork leg jerked behind him awkwardly.

Mama took Teddy and gave him the scolding Judith thought he deserved. Despite his squirmings, Mama refused to release him again. When he squalled, Mama ignored him.

"I'm definitely going to contact the electric company," Dr. Dan said. "I want my clinic to be electrified as soon as possible."

"Why?" Uncle Enoch said. "So you can look as ridiculous as these saloons?"

"The clinic is not a saloon," Dr. Dan said. "With electricity I'll be able to handle emergencies at any time of the day or night."

"That's what the hospital is for," Uncle Enoch muttered.

"Of course the hospital must be electrified, too," Dr. Dan said. "The next thing you'll want is electricity in your house."

Judith caught Abe's eye. She knew he was thinking that electric lights at home would be wonderful but that his father would never let electrical wires in the Stevenson household.

Abe turned to walk up Washington Avenue toward Hennepin. "Come on, let's go home."

"But they only turned on the lights a few minutes ago," Judith said. She was not finished looking at shop windows.

With slumped shoulders, Abe trudged up the street, moving against the crowd. Judith watched as he was swallowed up by the mass of onlookers.

CHAPTER 10

An Afternoon Escape

"Did you get enough to eat?" Aunt Tina asked.

Judith put her hand on her stomach. "I should have stopped ten minutes ago. But I love your bread, and I couldn't resist having more."

Abe slurped up the rest of his soup and let his spoon clatter in the dish. "I love a bowl of hot soup on a cold day."

"Thank you for making lunch, Aunt Tina," Judith said.

Abe pushed his empty bowl toward the center of the table. "Someday it won't be so much work to make lunch."

"It was just soup and bread," his mother said. "I would hardly call that a lot of work."

"Oh, yes it was," Abe insisted. "I saw you chopping potatoes and carrots half the morning. Someday there will be a machine to do that for you."

"I really don't mind doing it," Aunt Tina said as she carried dishes from the table to the sink.

"But there are so many other things you could be doing."

"Abe is right," Judith said. "You have lots of things you like to do. Why should you have to spend half your day in the kitchen preparing food?"

"Perhaps you have a point," Aunt Tina said. "It takes a long time to make bread, and it's such a mess. I wouldn't mind having a nice clean machine to do that."

"Someday it will happen," Abe said. "But first we have to get electricity in all the houses."

"Do you really think every family will have electric lights?" Judith asked.

"Electric lights are just the beginning, I'm sure of it. Someday I'm going to invent something to make life easier, and it's going to use electricity."

"What kind of machines are you thinking about?"

"There's no limit to the ideas," Abe said enthusiastically. "We could have machines to cook, machines to clean, even machines to travel in."

"It sounds like you've been reading more Jules Verne," his mother said.

"Jules Verne has lots of good ideas."

At the sound of a familiar shuffle, Judith turned toward the door and said, "Hello, Uncle Enoch."

"Are you hungry, Enoch?" Aunt Tina asked. "I haven't put the food away yet."

Uncle Enoch seemed not to hear his wife. His eyes were fixed on his son. Something about the way Uncle Enoch looked made Judith uncomfortable.

"Just remember, Abraham, that Mr. Verne writes fiction."

"I know, Papa, but real people could take his ideas and make them come true."

"You have to learn the difference between fiction and reality."

"Yes, Papa."

"Instead of sitting around dreaming about electric machines to help with the housework, you should be helping your mother with the dishes."

"Yes, Papa." Abe scraped his chair back. "I'll see if there's any hot water."

"It's plain as the nose on your face what electricity is going to do for those saloons," Uncle Enoch continued. "People will be down there drinking whiskey until all hours of the night."

"They already are," Aunt Tina remarked. "They used to use gas lamps; now they have electricity. How is it so different?"

"The electric lights make it seem like broad daylight in the middle of the night. It's not natural."

"Lots of things are not natural," Aunt Tina said. "Gas lamps are not natural, either. But we use them."

Abe stacked dishes at the side of the sink. Judith caught his eye. He had not said a word, leaving all the arguments for electricity to his mother.

"Uncle Enoch," Judith said. "I know you work late a lot of nights. Haven't you ever wished for better light so your eyes would not get so tired?"

Uncle Enoch glared at her, surprised that she would speak so bluntly.

"Young lady," he said, "you are just like your father. It doesn't take much for you to begin an argument."

Judith was about to object. She was not the one who had begun this discussion. But Aunt Tina's laughter stopped Judith's protest.

"I'm afraid he's right, Judith," Aunt Tina said. "Even when we were children, Charles always had to have the last word on everything."

"But, I—" Judith stopped in midsentence. Her aunt and uncle were looking at each other and smiling.

"See?" Aunt Tina said.

Judith clamped her mouth shut. Abe giggled quietly. At least something had cheered him up for the moment.

"Just remember, Abe," Uncle Enoch said, "help your mother. Don't sit around daydreaming all the time."

Judith was silent now. She liked her uncle Enoch. The other bankers thought he was very good at his job. His cautious, practical nature had saved the bank from disaster more than once. Businessmen all over Minneapolis wanted his advice. And she even believed he wanted the best for his son. So why did he have to be so harsh with Abe?

"Enoch," Aunt Tina said, as if she were reading Judith's mind, "Abe means no harm."

"There's no reason he can't be of more help around the house."

Abe filled the sink with water. He found a clean rag and began washing the lunch dishes.

"Do you want something to eat?" Aunt Tina repeated her earlier question.

Uncle Enoch shook his head. "I'm not hungry."

"Some coffee perhaps?"

"Yes, that would be nice."

"I'll bring you some in a few minutes."

Uncle Enoch shuffled out the way he had come.

Aunt Tina glanced at Judith and put a hand on Abe's shoulder. "We must try to understand your father," she said.

Abe whirled to face his mother. "But he doesn't try to understand me!" He threw the rag into the water with a slap.

"I know it seems that way," Aunt Tina said. "But I think he understands you better than you know."

Judith remembered her conversation with Uncle Enoch. *Even if he's going to be a scientist, he has to have his feet firmly on the ground,* Uncle Enoch had said. *As his father it's my job to provide guidance*. Judith had believed her uncle meant what he said. She looked at Abe's slumped shoulders. Obviously her cousin didn't know what to think about his father.

Abe started stacking clean dishes to one side of the sink.

Judith stood up. "I'll dry the dishes." She reached for a towel.

"Actually," Aunt Tina said, "I was hoping the two of you would go on an errand for me."

"What's that?" Abe asked.

"I'm nearly out of coffee, and I have a list of spices I need. Would you go down to Wagner's spice and coffee shop?"

"Downtown?" Abe's eyes lit up. "Can we look at the bridge while we're down there?"

"And the dress shop? Judith added.

Aunt Tina's eyes softened. "Certainly. Just don't dawdle all afternoon. I need the spices for supper."

"Yippee!" Abe plunged his hands into the dishwater.

His mother took the dishrag from him. "I'll finish here. You go on."

"What will Papa say?"

"Don't worry about your father. He's not so hardhearted as you think. Besides, he's the one who drinks the most coffee."

Abe shrugged his shoulders and looked at Judith. "Let's go!"

Judith tossed him a towel. "Dry off first."

A few blocks from the house, Abe sighed. "My father will never understand me." He was walking much slower than he usually did. Judith had no trouble keeping up with him.

"At least he notices you," Judith said. "He thinks of you enough to care about what you're doing."

"But I don't think he likes me very much," Abe said dejectedly. "The only way to make him like me is to give up all the things I care about—my experiments, my lab."

"He never said he wants you to do that."

"He doesn't have to say it," Abe muttered. "He wants me to

be a banker. Nothing else will make him happy."

"He just wants to protect you. Give him a chance."

Abe looked at Judith in surprise. "When I say that about your father, you get angry."

"It's different with my father."

"No, it's not."

"Yes, it is."

Abe kicked a rock. "Let's not argue."

Judith nodded in agreement. "I know what we need. We need an adventure."

Abe perked up. "They're getting ready to start construction on the stone arch bridge. We could go look at that."

Judith shook her head. "That's too real-life. You would just get depressed because your father does not approve of building a bridge for a railroad."

"What do you have in mind?"

"Something more imaginative. Let's pretend to be Swedish. If we meet anyone, we'll say *Göd middag* and *Tack sa mycket*."

"What does that mean?"

"Good afternoon and thank you very much."

Abe broke out laughing. "I have brown hair and brown eyes. You have red hair and green eyes. How in the world can we pretend to be Swedish?"

"If you can imagine electric machines for the future, you can imagine you are Swedish," Judith answered. "Mr. Johanssen's shop has the thread I need for my sampler. Let's go there."

Judith turned the corner and led the way.

Abe was laughing. "What else should I know about who we are?"

"We came from a farm outside Ursula in Sweden. Our parents brought us here so we could have a better life."

"The whole family?"

"We are the only children in the family. Our papa reads to us every night and answers all our questions about the new land."

"Can we have electricity in our house?"

"Of course. Our father is very progressive. That's why he came to a new country. We will receive a good education and grow up to be very successful."

"I think I like this."

They turned another corner.

"There's the shop," Judith said. "I need four colors."

"I don't want to go in that shop," Abe said. "Only women go in there. I'll wait outside."

"You're not ashamed to be Swedish, are you?" Judith grinned. "Our papa has taught us to be proud of who we are."

"Just go get your thread."

Judith disappeared inside. Abe leaned against the brick wall outside. Judith's last words echoed in his head. *Our papa has taught us to be proud of who we are.*

"Maybe your papa," Abe muttered. "Not mine." He wondered what his mother meant when she said Abe's father understood him better than he knew. His father did not understand him at all! Uncle Charles was the one who understood him. Uncle Charles knew how important science was and dreaming about the future without planning every little thing.

"All set." Judith reappeared with a little packet in one hand.

"My mother keeps asking me how far you are on that sampler," Abe said. "What should I tell her?"

"Tell her I'm on the third verse now, the part that says:

Neither life nor death shall ever,
  From the Lord His children sever,
Unto them His grace He showeth,
  And their sorrows all He knoweth."

And their sorrows all He knoweth, Abe thought. Did the heavenly Father know how he felt better than his earthly father did?

"I'll tell her," he murmured.

They walked a bit more.

"Here's the coffee shop," Abe said. "Let's make this fast so we have time to look at the bridge."

"You mean the dress shop," Judith teased.

Abe sighed and shook his head. "We used to like the same things. What happened?"

CHAPTER 11

A Disappointing Birthday

Judith braced herself in the living room, gripped the plate of cookies, and tried not to move. She was tempted to close her eyes until the rush was over. But she forced herself to keep them open in self-defense.

Papa had just opened the front door to let Dr. Dan and his family in. Richard squeezed past his parents and scampered into the living room. On the way in he dropped his coat in the entryway. Two-year-old Esther promptly tripped over her brother's coat. She let out a piercing wail as she fell to the wooden floor. Anna stopped to help her little sister up, all the while scowling at Richard's back.

Esther was back on her feet. "Teddy? Teddy?" she asked searchingly.

Judith looked down at Esther. "Mama just went upstairs to get Teddy up from his nap. He'll be down in a minute."

A minute was too long to wait. Anna and Esther zoomed toward the stairs.

Richard tugged on Judith's skirt. "I want Abe."

"You'll have to look for him," Judith said, still gripping the plate securely. "I don't know where he is."

Richard took a deep breath and screamed, "Abraham!"

"Richard!" Judith scolded. "I said you'll have to look for him."

"But I don't know where to look. If I call, he'll come to me."

"No screaming in the house," Judith warned. "Go look in the kitchen."

Pouting, Richard scuffled off toward the Fisk kitchen. Judith sighed and shook her head.

Papa came into the living room with Dr. Daniel and Aunt Marcia.

"Is everyone here?" Dr. Dan asked.

Judith nodded. "Aunt Tina is in the kitchen finishing the cake. Mama is upstairs. I'm not sure where Uncle Enoch and Abe are." To herself she added, *But I'm sure they are not together.*

Aunt Marcia had her children's coats in her hands. Now she wriggled out of her own coat and handed them all to Papa. "Fall is really here now," she said. "It's chillier every day."

"Enoch's birthday is always one of the hottest days of the year," Papa said. "And Abe and Judith's birthday is always cool."

Judith was twelve today. And for the twelfth year, the family was celebrating with a party that also honored Abe, who shared Judith's birthday.

"Here comes the birthday boy," Papa said cheerily as Abe entered the room.

Judith noticed that Papa had not said anything about the birthday girl.

"Mama says supper is almost ready," Abe announced.

79

"Good," Dr. Dan responded. "I'll just have a cookie to tide me over."

Judith realized she was still gripping the cookie plate so hard that her knuckles were turning white. She gladly handed the plate to Dr. Dan. He popped a sugar cookie in his mouth.

Papa reached for a cookie, saying, "I remember the party last year at your house, Abe. The gas lamps in the dining room stopped working, and we had to eat by candlelight."

"Maybe next year we can eat by electricity," Abe said.

Papa laughed. "Do you really think your father will change his mind about electricity in one year?"

"My father thinks I dream too much," Abe said. "I might as well dream about electricity in my house."

"That's certainly true," Papa agreed. "No matter what your father thinks, I hope you don't ever stop dreaming."

Judith watched the way her father looked at Abe. He was so proud of Abe. Why didn't he ever look at her that way? she wondered.

Mama came down the stairs just then with a sleepy Teddy in her arms. Anna and Esther thundered down right behind her.

Mama handed Teddy to Papa. "I'd better see if Tina needs help. After all, it is my kitchen."

"There's no need." Aunt Tina's voice came from the dining room. "We're ready to sit down and eat."

Judith saw that the traditional birthday dinner awaited them: ham with current sauce, boiled potatoes, corn pudding, green beans, and some of Aunt Tina's special dark bread. Judith liked everything except the green beans. Abe liked those, so Judith always agreed to have them on the menu.

"There you are!" Richard burst into the room and nearly tackled Abe.

Abe's sister Polly and Judith's brother Walter followed Richard in. "He was pestering us nearly to death about where you were, Abe."

"I was right here all the time."

"And now we're all here," Mama said.

Getting the younger children settled in their chairs took a few minutes. Judith breathed a sigh of relief when everyone was seated and Papa began to pray.

"Heavenly Father, we are grateful for the occasion that brings us together for this meal. Abe and Judith have blessed our family for the last twelve years, and it gives us great joy to celebrate this day. Be present with us and nourish us with this— Oomph!"

Papa's prayer broke off abruptly.

Judith opened her eyes in time to see her little brother pressing his head into Papa's stomach in an attempt to get into his lap.

"And Lord," her father continued, "thank You for the youngest blessing in the family. Amen."

Everyone laughed. No one was certain how Teddy had managed to climb down from his chair so quietly and quickly. But he had.

Smiling, Papa put Teddy back in his own chair. He glanced at Judith.

"I'll never forget the day you were born. We were so excited. Imagine our surprise when only a couple weeks later we received a letter from your aunt Tina telling us about Abe's birth."

"I'm glad they were born on the same day," Aunt Tina said. "It's like having twins—"

"In the family all over again." Judith and Abe finished the sentence in unison.

Papa and Aunt Tina said the same things every year. Judith put a spoonful of potatoes on her plate and listened politely for what she knew Papa would say next.

"The two of you are a lot like David and Daria: strong-spirited, independent, and inseparable."

Judith caught Abe's eye across the table. She was sure he was trying not to laugh. All of a sudden Judith wanted to giggle. She quickly stabbed a bit of ham and stuffed it in her mouth. That helped a little bit.

"Pass the bread, please," Aunt Tina said.

Judith picked up the bread basket and handed it to Walter, who passed it on to Aunt Tina.

"I remember when Daria was four and crossed a busy street all by herself," Aunt Tina said. "She wasn't afraid of anything."

"And David grew up to be the most stubborn child," Papa added.

Judith caught the glimmer in Abe's eye just before he spoke.

"Did you know he had his own baseball team for several years?" Abe said.

Papa looked at Abe with an odd expression. "Of course we know that."

Judith couldn't hold the laughter in any longer.

"Usually you say it," Abe explained to his uncle, grinning, "but I thought I would save you the trouble this year."

Papa and Aunt Tina joined Judith's laughter.

"Are we really so predictable?" Papa asked.

"Every year," Judith said, "on our birthday you tell us the same stories of Aunt Daria and Uncle David."

"Well, then, it's about time to change that tradition."

"Where's the cake?" Richard had barely touched his food, but he was anxious to move on to the heart of the celebration.

"Richard," Aunt Marcia said, "you must eat some corn pudding."

"But I want cake."

Mama stood up. "And you shall have cake, Richard. I'll go get it. You have just enough time to finish your corn pudding before I get back."

When Mama came back from the kitchen, she carried a large round cake with twelve candles glowing on top of it.

"Li, li," said Teddy, pointing with one chubby finger at the cake.

Judith and Abe were sitting across from each other. Mama set the cake down on the table between them.

"Li, li," Teddy repeated. He wriggled in his chair, trying to stand up.

"Are you ready to get down?" Papa asked. He lifted Teddy out of the chair and set him on the floor.

"You have to blow out the candles together," Mama said, "like you do every year. Blow at exactly the same moment."

Teddy was trying to climb into Abe's lap. "Li, li," he kept saying.

Abe swung the toddler into his lap.

"Are you ready, Judith?" Abe asked.

"Ready when you are."

"One," said Mama.

"Two." Everyone joined in the count.

"Li," said Teddy.

And he blew. Two of the candles went out.

Teddy stretched out a hand toward the remaining candles. Abe snatched him back just before he singed a finger. Instead, Teddy's fingers trailed through the frosting on one side of the cake. The heel of his hand caved in one edge.

"Teddy!" exclaimed Judith.

"He's all right," Papa said. "Abe's got him now."

Teddy sat in Abe's lap, staring at his fingers. He had been reaching for the candles, and instead he had a handful of frosting.

Papa laughed. "He doesn't know what he has on his fingers."

Experimentally, Teddy licked one finger. Then he put his whole hand in his mouth.

Papa roared. Mama was a little more sensible. She rescued Abe just before Teddy smeared a gooey hand across his cousin's face. With a rag, she wiped Teddy's fingers.

Judith looked forlornly at the cake. Two candles were out, three more were flickering.

"Let's relight the candles," she said.

"Never mind," Abe said. "Let's just blow out the rest."

"I want to relight them," she insisted.

"I think Abe is right," Mama said. "The candles are dripping too much wax. You'd better just blow."

Mama counted quickly this time. "One, two, three."

Judith blew half-heartedly. Abe put out most of the candles.

"Judith," Mama said, "why don't you cut the cake this year?"

Judith shrugged. "Abe can do it." She didn't want cake anymore.

Abe cut pieces for everyone, carefully avoiding the side of the cake that Teddy had raked his fingers through. He passed a piece to Judith. She did not touch it.

Papa started telling stories of the delightful and entertaining things Teddy had done recently. Judith fumed. Sharing her birthday with Abe was something she was used to. She even liked it. But she did not like sharing it with Theodore. He had his own birthday coming in a couple weeks. But everyone was acting like it was Teddy's birthday now.

Judith felt the familiar brush of Clover, her cat, against her ankle. Mama did not mind having Clover in the house, but she did not allow the cat at the dinner table. Judith would have to take him out. Bending over, she fished Clover out from under the table, then stood up to leave with him. Clover would need to be closed up in Judith's bedroom, or he would be right back in the dining room in less than two minutes.

On the stairs, Judith turned for a moment to look at the scene in the dining room. In the glow of the gas lamps, everyone was eating cake and laughing at Teddy.

No one will notice I'm gone, Judith thought. And she went upstairs to her room.

Once inside her room, Judith dumped Clover on the bed. She had intended to go back to the party, but suddenly she didn't feel like it. *They have Teddy,* she thought. *They don't need me.*

When she closed the door of her room to keep the cat in, Judith stayed inside, too.

Chapter 12

Judith Disappears

Abe knocked on the Fisk front door. He and Judith were going downtown to celebrate their first full day as twelve-year-olds. Their birthday had conveniently fallen on a Friday. They would be able to spend all of Saturday together.

Judith's mother opened the door. Teddy toddled behind her.

"Good morning, Aunt Alison," Abe said cheerily. He reached out and tousled Teddy's hair.

"Come on in," Aunt Alison said. "You're here bright and early. Did you enjoy last night's party?"

"Very much, thank you."

"I'm not sure Judith did," Aunt Alison said. "She didn't even eat any cake."

Abe had noticed that. "There are a lot of leftovers. She can have some today." Most of what was left was the part of the cake Teddy had smashed.

Abe did not want to worry his aunt. But he did think it was odd that Judith had disappeared from the party. At first he had thought she would be right back. But she had not returned. Even when it was time for Abe's family to go home, Judith was still upstairs. Abe was anxious to see her and make sure she was all right.

"Let me go find Judith," Aunt Alison said. "Come on, Teddy."

Abe sat down on a stair to wait. Aunt Alison was back in a few minutes with a puzzled look on her face. "I can't find Judith. She doesn't seem to be in the house."

Abe stood up. "Are you sure?"

"I've looked everywhere. She had breakfast about an hour ago. I haven't seen her since."

"Maybe she thought she was supposed to meet me on the bridge."

"She didn't say anything before she left."

"She's probably already downtown."

"Yes, perhaps that's it," Aunt Alison said, nodding.

"I'll go downtown," Abe said. His voice cracked. He hated that. He wished his voice would just finish changing. "If I don't come back soon, then you'll know I found her and we'll be back after lunch."

"I'm sure she's fine," Aunt Alison said. "It was just a mix-up in communication."

Abe raced downtown. Despite his aunt's calm words, he had a funny feeling about this. He and Judith never mixed up their communication. They understood each other perfectly, even when they did not talk.

Abe came to a halt at the end of the suspension bridge. Judith was not there. He scanned the other bridges. With her flaming red hair and green coat, she should be easily spotted. But he couldn't see her anywhere. Abe turned around to scour Bridge Square and the Washington Avenue shops.

Judith was not in the dress shop. She was not in the spice shop or Mr. Johanssen's yard goods store. Abe could not find Judith anywhere.

He raced back to the Fisk house and pounded on the door. Once again, his aunt opened it.

"Is Judith back?" he asked, panting.

Aunt Alison's eyes opened wide in alarm. "You didn't find her?"

Abe shook his head emphatically. "She wasn't in any of her favorite places."

"Perhaps you just missed her somewhere."

Again, Abe shook his head. "No. We were supposed to meet here. I'm sure of that. And if she'd gone downtown she would have waited for me at the end of the bridge."

"Charles!" Aunt Alison called. "Walter!" She flew into action. When her husband and son appeared, she explained what was wrong.

"I thought she was acting a bit strangely this morning," Uncle Charles said. "And it was odd that she disappeared the way she did last night during the party."

"I need some paper," Aunt Alison said. "We'll make a list of everywhere we should look."

"Let's not panic," Uncle Charles said. "Judith has been rather gloomy lately. She should not have gone off without telling us where she was going, but I'm sure she's fine."

"I want to be sure we don't miss anything," Aunt Alison insisted as she snatched up a scrap of paper. "Tell me again where you looked."

Abe verbally retraced the path he had taken that morning.

"We should double-check all those places in case you missed her," Uncle Charles said.

"And we should look in the attic," Aunt Alison added. "I didn't look there."

Abe dashed to the stairs. "I'll check the attic and the basement."

The attic was dark, and Abe had not thought to bring a lamp. Two small windows on either side of the house let in a spray of dim, dusty light. Abe had not been up in Judith's attic for a long time. But the shadows looked exactly the same as he remembered. He started to move around.

"Ow!" he cried out. Too late he remembered the stack of crates to one side of the stairs. Wincing, he reminded himself of the wardrobe and two chests on the other side. Gradually his eyes got used to the darkness. Nothing was disturbed, not even the dust. Judith was not there.

Abe took the stairs two at a time and zoomed down three flights to the basement. He saw rows of fruit preserves, jars of canned vegetables, and a pile of potatoes. But Judith was not there, either.

Upstairs again, Abe gave his report.

"Let's catch the streetcar," his uncle said, "and go downtown again."

"Stop by her friend Lucinda's house," Aunt Alison suggested. "Maybe she went there—or Catherine's."

"I wish you had a telephone," Abe muttered.

"It wouldn't help," Uncle Charles said. "Lucinda doesn't have one. The shops don't, either."

"Someday everyone will have a telephone."

"That may be an exaggeration. In any event, we don't have a telephone, so we have to do things the old-fashioned way, Mr. Verne."

"Go!" Aunt Alison said. "You're wasting time."

Uncle Charles and Abe hurried up the block and caught the streetcar. Abe hung out the open side, hoping to catch a glimpse of the dark green coat Judith usually wore. The streetcar rattled toward downtown, but it stopped much more often than Abe would have liked.

Judith, Abe thought, *what in the world are you doing? Why would you run off like this?*

Judith pulled her knees up to her chest and wished she had worn warmer stockings. It was time to change from cotton to wool. The sun had been shining when she left home three hours ago. She had not thought about how it would be where she was sitting now. A late October wind whistled right through her. She was tucked away from the warmth of the sun's rays, and her feet were getting cold. If only she had brought some hot tea.

No one knew where she was. Judith was sure of that. She would stay until she felt like going home, and that might not be for a long time. She might not even feel like going home that day at all. And since no one knew where she was, no one could make her go home.

Judith sighed. She supposed that she ought to go home before everyone started worrying about her. But she did not want to go home. Let them worry. Sometimes she got tired of always doing what she was supposed to do. Besides, as long as Teddy was toddling around the house, her parents would not miss her. And Walter did not pay much attention to her anyway.

She plunged her hands into the pockets of her warm green coat. A spray of water misted her face and sent a chill down her back. Judith knew she should get up and walk around; she would be much warmer. But she liked being hidden away. She would tolerate the cold while she tried to think of a warm place to move to without being seen.

"You're right, she's not here."

Judith's whole body jerked at the sound of Papa's voice. She turned her face upward in the direction of the sound and kept very still.

"I told you, I already looked here."

Abe was with Papa! And there were looking for her.

Judith sat like a stone.

"Aunt Alison thinks Judith ran away, doesn't she?" Abe asked.

"She may think that," Papa said. "But I don't think so."

"She's twelve," Abe said. "And she's too smart to really run away."

"I think you're right. She just needs to think."

Judith felt a sneeze coming. She was determined to stifle it. Papa and Abe were too close.

"Let's try the thread shop again," Abe said. He did not really think they would find Judith there, but they had to do something besides stand in the street and talk.

Once they were gone, Judith let herself sneeze freely—three times. She definitely felt cold and wet. But Papa and Abe were gone. She could relax again.

"Abe," Uncle Charles said, "we'll have to split up. I'm going to go to Lucinda's house. You try Dr. Dan's."

"Why would she go to Dr. Dan's?" Abe asked doubtfully.

"Why would she go anywhere?" Uncle Charles countered. "We'll have to ask Judith, but first we have to find her."

Abe sighed. "Okay. I'll look at Dr. Dan's."

As Abe suspected, Dr. Dan and Aunt Marcia had not seen Judith.

"I haven't seen her since we cut the cake last night," Dr. Dan said. "Why would she leave her own party like that?"

That was the question everyone was asking. Abe had no answer.

Next he decided to try his own house. Maybe Judith would eventually go there looking for him. No streetcar was passing by just then. Abe had to walk.

By now it was almost lunchtime. Abe had spent his entire Saturday morning looking for someone who was not lost. No matter what Aunt Alison thought, Abe was sure Judith would be back before nightfall.

But suppose she wasn't? If she was upset enough to leave her own party without eating birthday cake, she might be upset enough to stay away from home. Abe could not take that chance.

He had to find Judith. He knew her better than anyone else. He should be able to figure out where she would go when she was mad. Why hadn't he figured it out yet?

Abe stopped by his house and swallowed a sandwich made from the leftovers of last night's ham. Before leaving again, he checked his lab out back. It was empty and welcoming. For a moment, he considered staying in the lab to work. He wouldn't have to stay long, he told himself, just for a few minutes. But then he told himself that, like Judith, he was twelve years old now. He should act responsibly—even if Judith did not.

Abe told his mother what was going on. Then, with steps slowed by fatigue, he trudged back to Judith's house to see if Uncle Charles had had any success.

The answer was no. Lucinda had given Judith a scarf as a birthday present two days ago and had not spoken to her since. Catherine and Judith had had a tiff five days ago. Judith would surely not go there.

Abe sank into a chair and sighed.

"Think," his uncle Charles urged. "Where else would Judith go? Where would she go if she just wanted to be by herself for a while?"

In the pocket on the left side of her coat was a small packet. Judith knew what it was without looking at it. It held four skeins of thread for her sampler. She had not worked on the project much lately. She tried to remember where she was.

God His own doth tend and nourish,
In His holy courts they flourish,
From all evil things He spares them,
In His mighty arms He bears them.

Neither life nor death shall ever
From the Lord His children sever;

Unto them His grace He showeth,
  And their sorrows all He knoweth.

If only she could believe she was in the care of such a father, Judith thought. She felt a tiny bit guilty for not making herself known when Papa and Abe had come looking for her. She had to admit that Papa sounded genuinely concerned. Mama thought she had run off. At least Papa knew her well enough to know she would not do that. Even so, she was surprised he had come looking for her.

"I know!" Abe jumped up out of his chair, nearly dumping Teddy on the floor. "I know where she is!"

"Where?" Aunt Alison asked.

"Let's go," Uncle Charles said.

Abe shook his head. "No, I should go by myself. But I'm sure she's there."

He left before they could say anything more.

Chapter 13
The Answer

Now Abe had the energy to run. Now he knew where he was going. He passed all the familiar places that he had already passed several times that day. He scolded himself: *What took you so long to think of it?* He knew exactly where to find Judith. It was a place Uncle Charles and Aunt Alison would never think of. Or at least it would be another two days before they would think to look there.

Abe ran even faster. He was too impatient to look for a streetcar. He would save the coins he had for the ride home with Judith.

Judith's stomach snarled and growled. The bread and cheese she had fed it two hours ago had already worn off. She still had an apple and a chicken leg, but she was planning to have that for her supper. Then she would have to make a decision about going home. If she could manage to ignore the cramp that was developing in her stomach, she could delay that decision for another four or five hours.

She was getting cramps in her legs, too. In order to stay balanced on her ledge, she had to keep her knees up under her chin most of the time. Judith ached to stretch out her legs, but she was not ready to come out of hiding.

The wind carried a spray of water to her face. Judith shivered. Her coat was damp now. But she was not going home.

Abe was almost there. He paused at the end of the bridge to look for evidence that Judith had come this way. He had been at this spot twice already that day looking for Judith on the bridge. It had taken him until the middle of the afternoon to realize he should look for her under the bridge.

The pavement of the bridge yielded to a dirt path that curved around and ducked under the bridge. Abe had been there with Judith seven or eight times before. And every time she had remarked that it felt like a different world, a place where she could forget about the things that bothered her. So of course Judith would come here now.

Abe balanced himself against the brick tower that held up one end of the bridge and slid slightly downhill. As he did, he was sure he caught a glimpse of the green coat he had been looking for all day. Quietly, carefully, he moved toward Judith along the rocky slope. Her eyes were fixed straight ahead, out over the river. She did not see him coming until he was at her ledge.

Crouching next to her, he said, "Hello, Judith."

She turned to him and did not speak.

"You look cold," he said.

"I am," she admitted reluctantly.

"Why didn't you wait for me this morning?" Abe said. "I would have come here with you instead of going downtown."

"I guess I felt like being by myself," Judith said.

"You always said that being with me was just as good as being alone," Abe said. "When did that change?"

"I guess it hasn't. You found me and I'm not mad. Actually, I'm glad to see you."

Abe nudged her. "Then make room for me to sit next to you."

Judith inched over as far as she dared, and Abe squeezed in beside her.

"We're getting too big for this," Abe remarked.

"I wasn't planning on needing room for you when I came here."

"Just what were you planning, Judith?" Abe asked quietly.

"I'm hungry, I'm cold, and you found me," Judith answered. "I guess that means I didn't plan anything very well. It was a spontaneous decision."

Abe pointed to the view. "It's a beautiful place to be spontaneous."

"Your father would not approve," Judith said.

Abe laughed.

From the refuge under the bridge, they looked out on the surging river below. Foaming white blasts of water pounded over the St. Anthony Falls. When the wind was just right, frigid droplets sprayed their faces and left a momentary dampness on the rocks around them. At the base of the mighty falls, water swirled in tight circles and gave in to the southward flow of the powerful Mississippi.

Across the river was the Pillsbury A mill and assorted railroad cars. All around Judith's hideaway, Minneapolis bustled.

"I've been watching the water all day," Judith said. "It just keeps coming. Where does it all come from, and where does it all go?"

"The Mississippi River originates in—"

Judith cut off Abe's geography lecture. "I know the facts," she said. "I was in Miss Redmond's fourth grade class with you, remember?"

"Then why did you ask the question?"

"It was one of those questions you are not really supposed to answer."

"Rhetorical?"

"That's the kind. We take the river for granted, and we think the falls will always be there."

"Of course they will be," Abe said.

Judith shook her head. "You can't be sure of that, not absolutely certain. Don't forget what happened in 1873. Someone tried to dig a tunnel under the falls and nearly destroyed them."

"That was a special case. Humans tried to interfere with nature."

"But it proves that anything can change, even the river."

Abe looked at the falls. It was hard to imagine how they could ever disappear. But he did not argue with Judith. Somehow, he thought, she was leading up to something. He would just wait.

"For eleven years," Judith said, "it was Mama and Papa and Walter and me. It was a comfortable family. I liked it that way. I knew where I fit in."

"And now?"

"Now there is Teddy."

"And?"

"This is a hateful thing to say, but I'm jealous of Teddy."

Abe turned his head away so Judith could not see his smile. She was finally admitting something that he had known for a long time.

"Don't misunderstand me," Judith said. "Teddy is my little brother, and I love him. But everything turned upside down when he was born."

"What do you mean?"

"Papa thinks about Teddy all the time. He doesn't pay any attention to me anymore."

"Teddy is a baby. Babies take a lot of work. Probably when

you were a baby your father was the same way with you."

Judith fingered the packet of thread in her coat pocket.

"Maybe he was. I don't remember that. I only remember now. And now Papa is more interested in Teddy and you than he is in me."

"Me?" Abe said in surprise. "I thought we were talking about Teddy."

"Papa pays just as much attention to you as he does to Teddy. He always wants to know about your experiments and visits you in your lab."

"So? We're interested in the same things—friends."

Judith shook her red curls. "No, it's more than common interests. Papa is interested in you. He would be no matter what things you liked."

"Your father is interested in you, too," Abe said.

"He never asks to see my sampler. I've been working hard on that for months."

"He knows you're working on a sampler."

"But he never looks at it. I don't think he even knows what it says. Sometimes he tries to be interested in me, but he doesn't know what to say. Why is it so hard?"

Abe slumped back against the stone wall. "You always tell me that my father is trying to help me. But it doesn't seem that way to me. He never looks at my experiments."

"Uncle Enoch may not approve of your experiments, but at least he cares about them enough to have an opinion. He has his reasons for making sure you don't get carried away with your experiments. He pays more attention than you think."

"And your father spent most of the day looking for you."

"I know."

"Your mother is pretty worried, too."

"You don't have to keep saying things to make me feel worse."

"I promised her I would bring you home."

"You shouldn't make promises you can't keep."

"I think I can keep this one. I don't think you were really planning to run away."

"How can you be so sure?"

"The cat. You would never leave Clover behind if you meant to be gone for good."

"Want an apple? Or a chicken leg?"

"Huh?" Abe did not know why Judith suddenly was talking about food.

Judith chuckled. "That's all the food I have left. When it's gone, I have to go home."

"There's a lot of birthday cake left."

"With a big fat handprint in it!"

They laughed.

Then Judith groaned. "How will I explain all this to my parents?"

Abe pointed at the thundering falls. "Just think about that."

Judith followed his finger, but she looked puzzled.

"You said your family was like the river," Abe said. "It still is. Running off today won't change that."

Judith considered her cousin for a moment. "I feel silly for what I did."

"The main question is, do you feel better than you did last night?"

Judith nodded slowly. "I suppose so."

"Are you ready to go home?"

Abe and Judith hopped off the streetcar two blocks from her home. Her stomach fluttered uncontrollably. She still had no idea how she could explain her thoughtless behavior to her parents. Judith did not feel like her thirteenth year was getting off to a very good start.

"Are you coming in with me?" Judith asked Abe.

He shrugged. "If you want me to."

"What am I going to say?"

"I have a feeling you won't have to say very much."

As they walked up the porch steps, the front door flew open and the rest of Judith's family burst out. Papa was first, with Teddy in his arms, and Walter and Mama behind him.

As soon as he saw Judith, Papa turned around and handed Teddy to Walter. Teddy protested, but Papa paid no attention. Instead, he turned to Judith and opened his arms wide.

The School Bully

"So Uncle Charles didn't scold you at all for running off on Saturday?"

After seeing Judith home, Abe had not stayed long at the Fisk house. Judith needed to be alone with her parents, he thought. But he was curious about what happened after he left. So he questioned Judith on the way to school on Monday.

"I tried to apologize," Judith said. "I knew I had worried them half to death by disappearing like that. But Papa wouldn't hear of it. He wouldn't even let me say I was sorry."

"I told you it would be all right to go home," Abe said.

"He just wanted to know how I was," Judith continued. "Was I warm enough, did I need something to eat, things like that. My mother took Teddy out of the room, and it was just Papa and me. And do you know, we didn't have any trouble talking. We haven't talked like that for a long time—since before Teddy was born."

"Did you tell him everything—how you were feeling and why you ran off to the bridge?"

Judith nodded, smiling. "And he understood. I didn't think he would, but he did. He even asked to see my sampler."

"Did he like it?"

"He said it's one of his favorite hymns—the same thing Mama says."

"I'm really glad to hear everything went so well."

"I felt like he wanted to have a party just because I came home. He didn't care how silly it was of me to go off in the first place. We ate leftover birthday cake. Walter thought I should be scolded, but Papa said he wanted to celebrate that I was back, safe and sound. Mama made a big dinner, with pot roast and glazed carrots and a pie."

"I saw you sitting in church with your father yesterday," Abe said. "You were sharing a hymnal, and you looked very happy."

"I was. It was the first time in a long time that I wasn't wondering what my parents thought about me. When Teddy got fussy, Papa sent Walter out with him. They usually want me to take Teddy out. My parents stayed all the way through the service with me."

"I noticed that."

"What about you?" Judith asked.

"What about me?"

"I saw you in church yesterday, too, silly. And you didn't look quite as miserable as you usually do sitting next to your father."

"Suppose I said I didn't feel miserable, either?"

Judith slowed her step. "Did you talk to your father?"

"After I left your house, I thought about what you had said while we were sitting under the bridge."

"What did I say?"

"That my father wants what is best for me. That he takes his job of being a father very seriously. I had never thought of it that way before."

"So what did you do while I was stuffing myself with smashed leftover cake?"

Abe shrugged one shoulder. "I asked him some questions about the bank during dinner. That seemed to please him. I haven't seen him that excited in a long time. And my mother was really happy to see the two of us talking."

"Did you really want to know about the bank?" Judith was skeptical but curious.

"Well, not at first. But I have to admit, it was interesting after he got started talking. I said I thought that banking was like scientific experiments in some ways."

"How?"

Abe laughed. "That's what my father wanted to know. He didn't criticize my idea just because it was about science."

"So what did you say?"

"You start out with a theory of what you think is true. Then you try to prove it by controlling the circumstances and making certain things happen."

"Banking is like that?"

"Sure. You think certain investments will make money if you manage them just right. You can predict pretty accurately how many people will pay back their loans every year, and so on."

"It sounds like you talked about banking for a long time."

Abe smiled. "Longer than I would have predicted when I asked my first question. Mama was finishing the dishes and we were still talking. My father says that when I'm sixteen I can have an after-school job at the bank if I want it."

"So now you're going to be a banker?"

"I didn't say that. But how can I expect my father to understand my science if I don't try to understand what he does for a living? I want to be fair."

"Hey, Abe!"

Abe snapped his head around to answer the voice behind him. "Catch!"

A baseball came flying through the air. Judith ducked. Abe reached up and snatched the ball out of the air.

"Hello, Stephen," Abe said to his friend. He lobbed the ball back to Stephen.

"Been playing much ball lately?" Stephen asked, catching up with Abe and Judith just outside the schoolyard.

"Nah," Abe answered. "It's getting too cold."

Judith snorted. "The cold never seems to bother you when you're in your lab. You go out there all the time in the winter."

"That's different." Abe swung his bundle of books to his other shoulder. "That's work. You can't stop working just because it gets cold. Someday someone will invent a way to keep a building like the lab warm."

"If you built a fire in there, you'd burn the place down," Judith observed.

"But electricity is hot," countered Abe. "There may be a way to heat a room that way."

"If you want to be a professional baseball player," Stephen said, "you can't stop playing ball just because it gets cold."

"Is that what you want?" Judith asked. "To be a professional baseball player?"

"Why not? I'm really good. Everybody says so."

Judith snickered. "And you're one of the humblest people I've ever known, too."

Stephen scowled. They went through the gate into the schoolyard. The mornings were chilly and damp now. Most students arrived at school in their warmest coats. Judith had started wearing her wool stockings every day.

From behind them came a shuffling sound. What was Father doing at the schoolyard? Abe turned around.

But it was not Father. It was Christopher Harrod. With a sneer, he dragged one leg lamely behind him, leaving a trail in the dirt.

"What are you doing, Christopher?" Stephen snapped.

"Abe knows what I'm doing, don't you, Abe?" Christopher leaned way to the left and dragged his right foot forward.

"You're acting like an idiot," Stephen said. "Abe knows that. We all do."

Judith looked stunned. Christopher's imitation of Abe's father was perfect. It was as if he had been practicing for a long time. But why would he do that?

"I heard what you were saying about being a baseball player," Christopher said to Stephen. "It's a good thing you have two good legs. Otherwise, you might end up having to be a banker."

"There's nothing wrong with being a banker," Abe said evenly. He felt the color rising in his face. "It has nothing to do with how well your legs work."

"Do you really think that sour old man at the bank could be anything but a banker?" Christopher taunted. "I've seen him get on a streetcar. It takes him twice as long as a normal person."

"My father is normal," Abe said, his voice rising to match the redness in his cheeks. "He is not a sour old man."

Judith put a hand on Abe's arm. "Just ignore him," she said. "Let him get past us."

Christopher scoffed. "Admit it, Abe. Even you think your father is weird."

Abe clenched his fists.

With his eyes boring into Abe, Christopher dragged his foot forward a few more inches.

"Maybe I'll call this the banker's walk," Christopher sneered.

"There is nothing wrong with being a banker," Abe repeated. "You have to be very smart to be a banker."

Christopher laughed rudely. "At least it's a job you can do sitting down."

"Don't pay any attention," Judith said. "He'll go away."

Abe looked around. The schoolyard was filling up now. The bell would ring soon. But until it did, students would continue gathering to watch the showdown. More than a dozen already had slowed their steps to remain near Abe and Christopher. Their eyes reflected their curiosity.

Abe swallowed hard. He wanted to take Judith's advice and ignore Christopher Harrod. But how could he stand by and watch someone ridicule his father?

Christopher's gray eyes taunted Abe. The circle around them grew larger. At least twenty other students were watching.

"Just go away, Christopher," Stephen said. "Leave Abe alone."

"Are you going to fight his battles?" Christopher asked.

"There is no battle," Stephen said. "There's just you making a fool of yourself in front of everybody."

"Is that right? Then why is Abe so red in the face? Why are his eyes sticking out like that?"

Abe's shoulders were so stiff he could hardly feel them. His head pounded, and he was sweating even though the morning was cold. He looked around at the growing audience watching to see what he would do next. None of them would blame him if he lunged at Christopher Harrod and beat the stuffing out of him. In fact, they would probably cheer him on. But would that stop anyone from making fun of his father again?

Abruptly Abe spun around and started walking toward the school. Judith and Stephen immediately fell into step beside him.

The taunting shuffle continued behind them. Abe refused to turn around and look. After a few more steps, it was gone.

"You did the right thing," Judith told Abe.

"I'm still not sure," Abe answered. "Maybe I should have defended my father."

"You did defend your father," Judith said.

"Not very well. Christopher Harrod will do the same thing another day, I'm sure of that."

"You have to ignore him," Stephen insisted. "If he can't make you mad, he'll move on."

"Right," Abe said. "He'll move on to make fun of someone else's father."

Inside the school, Abe sat across the classroom from Christopher Harrod. Christopher wadded up bits of paper and spit them across the aisle. He never had his book open to the right page. And when the teacher called on him, he never even knew what the question was. He certainly did not know the answer.

How could someone as obnoxious as Christopher Harrod make him feel such deep feelings? Abe wondered. But he had.

CHAPTER 15

Midnight Adventure

"Be careful," Judith hissed.

"I can't see anything!" Abe responded in a hoarse whisper.

"You've been in my house a million times," Judith whispered back. "You know where all the furniture is."

A thud followed by a moan told Judith that Abe's toe had just found the leg of the kitchen table.

"Shhh!" she said.

"I'm in pain!"

"Shhh!"

Judith felt something fuzzy brush against her ankle. "Watch the cat," she whispered.

"Meow!"

It was too late. Abe jumped off Clover's tail as the cat turned and snarled at him.

Judith scooped up Clover and did her best to soothe him. Abe froze where he stood and held his breath. They listened for the sound of a step on the stairs. None came. Finally Abe let himself breathe.

"Go back to sleep, Clover," Judith said quietly as she set the cat down on the floor—away from Abe.

"I'm hungry," Abe said.

"Now?" Judith could not believe Abe was talking about food at such a time.

"I can't help it. Getting up in the middle of the night always makes me hungry."

"How often do you do this?" Judith reached for the fruit bowl on the kitchen table and stuck a couple apples in her coat pocket. "Now we're ready."

Judith groped for the back door. Stealthily, she turned the handle. The door creaked open and she slipped out. Abe was right behind her.

"Do you think they heard anything?" Abe asked. He no longer whispered. "That back door is noisy."

"Quiet!" Judith hushed him. She pointed to her parents' bedroom window up above them.

They moved away from the house with careful, silent steps. Abe repeated his question.

Judith glanced back over her shoulder. Her parents' window remained dark. They had not gotten up to light a candle or the gas lamp next to the bed.

"Ever since Teddy started sleeping through the night better, my parents never wake up during the night," she said.

"That's a relief."

"I would never have agreed to this if I thought they might wake up."

"I'm glad you did agree."

"Are you sure Walter didn't hear you get up?" Judith asked. Abe was supposed to be spending the night at her house, sleeping in the bed next to her brother's.

Abe shook his head. "He never moved a muscle. That guy sleeps like a log."

They moved out into the night and wound their way along the familiar path that would take them downtown. It was midnight, and the sky was black.

The two cousins had thought the spring of 1883 would never come. In January, even Abe had admitted that it was too cold to be out in his lab. Now, at the end of April, it was finally starting to warm up. Judith only hoped that Mama, Papa, Walter, and Teddy would stay asleep. Clover was the only one to see them leave, and he couldn't talk. Judith was sure the cat was sound asleep again by now, too.

"It's cold out here," Judith remarked. The dampness of the spring night air tickled her nostrils.

"You have the blood of a frog," Abe said. But he buttoned his coat under his neck.

"There won't be any streetcars at this hour of the night."

"No. We'll have to walk the whole way."

They headed in the familiar direction of Hennepin Avenue, which would take them across Washington and on to the bridge—and Bridge Square.

Despite Uncle Enoch's doubts, electricity was spreading in the downtown area of Minneapolis. Only a few months after the shops and saloons on Washington Avenue were electrified, Bridge Square got its first lights. Abe and Judith wanted to see them shine against the black night sky.

"Can you see the lights?" Abe said enthusiastically in full voice. They were only a few blocks from Bridge Square.

"Yes!"

Ahead of them, a circle of lights rose high in the sky and seemed to hang from nothing.

"This was sure worth getting up in the middle of the night," Abe said.

"It's like a crown of jewels on black satin," Judith pronounced.

"Only a girl would think that."

"What do you see?"

Abe tilted his head and squinted at the lights. "It's bursts of electricity circling around and creating a current."

"Only a scientist would see that," Judith retorted. "How high is it?"

"It's 257 feet high," Abe said proudly.

"Can we go up to that platform?" Judith had seen people up in the light mast during the day.

"I haven't figured out how to get up there," Abe said. "Besides, someone might see us."

They crossed Washington Avenue. The street was nearly empty. Occasionally the door of one of the saloons opened and someone came out.

"Look at these electric arm lamps," Abe said. "We watched the electric company workers install them, but I never imagined they would look this spectacular at night."

"There's an electric lamp right outside your father's bank," Judith observed.

Abe groaned. "He was not happy when they put that in. But the bank president thinks it's a good idea."

Judith raised her eyes once again to the enormous light fixture ahead of them.

"I can see shadows all the way down here," she said.

"Let's go stand under the light mast," Abe said, and he strode as fast as his long legs would carry him. Judith quickened her pace to catch up, just as she always did when Abe got excited about something.

Soon they stood under the great light mast itself. The ring of lights towered above them. Eight huge lamps lit up the Bridge Square area. Hanging her head back to look up at them, Judith started to feel dizzy.

"It's not a crown or electricity," Judith said. "It's a moon, our very own moon just for Minneapolis."

"It's so bright!" Abe said, amazed. "They can probably see it in St. Paul."

"Look at City Hall," Judith said, pointing. "People could work in their offices right now and not need a lamp."

She turned around and realized that Abe was no longer beside her.

"Where are you going?" she asked, trailing after him.

"Down closer to the water," he answered. "The light must be reflecting down there, too."

"Be careful, Abe." Judith was not convinced they should leave the safety of the Bridge Square area. But Abe had already trotted off ahead of her, so she followed.

"Look at the stone arch bridge," Abe said, pointing downstream. The bridge, under construction and nearly finished, curved over the falls in a series of arches. The other bridges were suspended over the river. This one, built to support the weight of a train, was rooted deeply in the riverbed.

"They've made a lot of progress in the last few weeks," Judith observed. "There's only a little bit left to go."

"Yep, and then the trains from the Great Northern Railroad can come right across the river."

At the end of the suspension bridge, Abe leaned over one side and said, "That's where you hid out after our birthday, remember?"

"How could I forget? Walter reminds me about it constantly."

"You stopped complaining about your father after that."

"Papa and I understand each other better, now."

"Well, then, something good came out of it." He leaned over a few inches more.

111

"Be careful, Abe!"

"I wonder if we can still fit down there," he said. "We haven't grown that much since October."

"Abe, don't be ridiculous. We can't go down there. In fact, we should probably get home pretty soon." Judith started moving away from the end of the bridge.

"I know. I just wanted to see the water. Do you remember how magnificent the river looked from under the bridge?" He moved around the edge, looking for the path that curved around under the bridge.

Suddenly he dropped to the ground.

"Abe!" Judith spun around and groped in the darkness for her cousin's hand.

"I'm here," Abe responded. "I just slipped in the mud."

"Are you all right?"

"I'm going to have a hard time explaining the condition of my clothes in the morning. Pull me up."

Judith held on to the bridge's supporting tower with one hand and reached out with the other hand. She felt the pull of Abe's weight.

"Let go!" she cried. She knew she could no longer hold her balance on the slippery ground.

It was too late. Her feet went out from under her, and she plopped down in the mud.

Abe roared with laughter.

"What's so funny?" Judith said, irritated. "If you hadn't come down here in the first place, I wouldn't be covered with mud."

Abe succeeded in pulling himself up and climbed toward Judith. Then he extended his hand and helped her to her feet. They moved cautiously to solid ground.

In the light of the electric arcs, they examined each other. Judith had a handkerchief in her coat pocket, but they needed much more than a scrap of white cotton to clean themselves off. Abe had fallen on his side. Mud streaked his clothing from knee to shoulder. The back of Judith's dress and coat were soaked.

"I think we're in trouble now," Abe said. For the first time that night, he sounded worried about the consequences of their escapade.

"We've been up half the night down here," Judith said. "Now we'll be up the other half of the night trying to get our clothes clean."

"But that will make too much noise," Abe protested as he started to walk back up toward Washington Avenue.

"Maybe we can just stuff our clothes away, put on something clean, and wash them out another time."

"That will work for you," Abe said. "But I'm only spending one night at your house. I didn't bring any other clothes."

Judith groaned. "I could get you something of Walter's, but that would make everyone ask questions."

"We've got to find a way to clean up tonight."

They discussed the possibilities all the way home. But they need not have bothered.

"Oh, no," Judith groaned, when she saw a light burning in her family's kitchen.

"Maybe they don't know we're gone," Abe said. "Maybe your father couldn't sleep and got up to have some warm milk."

"I suppose so."

"We can just wait outside until he goes back upstairs."

"But it's freezing out here, and we're soaking in mud."

"Do you really want to go in there?" Abe said.

Judith scowled as she considered her options. They were close to the house now. They would have to make a decision soon. Quietly, they moved around to the side of the house.

They didn't move fast enough. The back door opened. Papa loomed over them.

Abe and Judith looked at each other with sinking stomachs.

"I hope you enjoyed your outing," Papa said calmly, "because there will not be another one for a very, very long time."

CHAPTER 16
Interrupted Plans

Judith didn't bother to knock on the door to Abe's lab. She just yanked it open and entered.

He looked up, surprised. "What are you doing here?"

"My mother came over to see your mother. I couldn't believe it when she said I could come with her." Judith perched on the barrel and looked around the lab. More than two weeks had passed since she had been inside it. "I'm so glad to get out of the house that I'm even glad to see your lab."

"I know what you mean," Abe said, pushing a beaker aside. "I can't believe they won't let us go anywhere except school and church for a whole month."

"Only two more weeks now," Judith muttered. "At least you've got your lab."

"At first my father wouldn't even allow me to come out here," Abe said. "He only changed his mind two days ago."

"It sounds like your parents were just as angry as mine."

"I've never seen my father so red in the face," Abe said. "He wanted to put me on restriction for three months."

"Three months!"

"My mother said it had to be the same punishment you had."

"So now we have to waste another whole Saturday," Judith lamented.

"What have you been doing?"

"I've nearly finished my sampler," Judith answered. "And I'm ahead in my schoolwork. How about you?"

"I've stayed in my room a lot reading a Jules Verne book."

"You didn't want your father to see you reading it, did you?"

Abe shook his head and turned back to his workbench.

"I don't think the punishment fits the crime," Judith blurted out. "We were only gone a couple hours. Why should we have to stay home for a whole month?"

Abe shrugged. "My mother says that when I'm a parent, I'll understand their decision."

Judith frowned. "I hate it when parents say things like that."

"We're not children anymore," Abe said, his voice cracking. He tried to control it. "We've been allowed to go downtown by ourselves in the daytime for a long time. Is it really so different at night?"

"That's what I asked Papa," Judith said. "He wouldn't even talk about it. He just told me to go to my room and try to think like an adult instead of a selfish child. I am not a selfish child!"

Abe leaned his elbows on the workbench behind him and considered their dilemma. "Do you think they would have let us go if we had asked permission?"

Judith sighed. "I don't know. I guess we'll never find out now."

Abe agreed. "We don't dare suggest anything like that for a long time."

"I'm sorry that we upset our folks," Judith said, "but it was a beautiful sight!"

"I have to agree with that. It was almost worth the trouble we're in." Abe glanced out the lab's little window toward the house. "Why did your mother come over here? Is Teddy with you?"

"Yes, Teddy's here," Judith said, moaning slightly. "Papa and Walter are busy. Mama said it was a nice spring afternoon and that we shouldn't waste it in the house. So we went for a walk and ended up here."

Judith saw the back door of the house open. Mama's head appeared.

"Abe! Judith!"

"What did we do now?" Abe asked.

"We'd better answer right away." Judith hopped off the barrel and pushed open the door. Mama met them in the yard.

"Tina and I have decided to go downtown for a little while," Mama said.

Judith's thoughts surged—downtown!

"Since the two of you are not allowed to go," Mama continued, "we'll leave Teddy here with you."

"But Aunt Alison," Abe protested, "I'm working in my lab."

"You'll have to come back to the house," Mama said firmly. "We'll only be gone a couple hours."

"What about Polly?" Judith asked.

"She's coming with us," Mama answered.

"But Mama—"

"It won't be as difficult as you think," Mama said. "It's almost time for Teddy's nap. I brought his favorite blanket along. Just put him down on a bed upstairs."

"But he doesn't like to sleep in strange places."

"This is not a strange place. He's napped here many times."

Mama turned and went back in the house. Reluctantly, Judith followed. Teddy was sitting on a stool at the kitchen table eating a snack. Mama, Aunt Tina, and Polly left shortly after that. Abe and Judith were left watching Teddy stuff raisins into his mouth.

"Down," Teddy said.

Judith lifted him off the stool and set him on the floor. "It's almost time for your nap," she told him.

"No nap!" Teddy zoomed out of the kitchen and ran wildly into the living room.

"Teddy, no!" Judith said, chasing him. "No running in the house."

Teddy hurled himself into a sofa, head first. "Play, play!"

"After your nap." Judith turned to Abe, behind her. "Help me, Abe."

"He's your brother," Abe said. "I don't know how to put him down for a nap."

"He likes you. You can get him to calm down."

Abe shrugged. "I'll try."

He crossed the room to the sofa and sat beside Teddy. The little boy stood up on a cushion and patted Abe's head. "Up, up."

"All right," Abe said. He stood up and swung Teddy up onto his shoulders. Then he headed for the stairs.

"Smart thinking," Judith said. She followed him up the stairs with Teddy's tattered blue blanket looped over one arm. "Let's try putting him down on your bed. He likes it in there."

"I don't want him messing with my things."

"He won't. He'll be sleeping."

"Promise?"

"Let's at least try."

Abe deposited Teddy on his bed and wrestled to get the toddler to lie down. Judith tucked the blanket around him.

"He likes it when Mama sings," Judith said.

"So sing."

"You sing."

"I won't sound like your mother," Abe argued. "You sing."

Judith tried to remember the melody she often heard Mama singing to Teddy. It was the same one Mama had sung to Judith when she was younger. Slowly the tune came to her head and she began to hum.

Teddy found his thumb and rolled his head to one side. Judith kept humming. Abe crept out of the room. Judith hummed some more.

Downstairs a few minutes later, Abe and Judith were quite pleased.

"That was easier than I thought," Judith admitted.

"At least it will be peaceful for a while."

"What do you want to do now?"

"Something quiet."

"We could play checkers."

"More sing," a little voice demanded.

They turned around and saw Teddy standing at the top of the stairs, dragging his blanket behind him.

"More sing," he repeated.

Judith sighed. "All right, Teddy. I'll sing some more."

Abe waited for her downstairs with a book by Jules Verne in his lap, *The Mysterious Island*. He waited a long time. By the time Judith appeared again, Abe had finished a whole chapter.

"Is he really asleep this time?"

Judith nodded. "I'm sure he'll sleep at least two hours now."

"Good. Let's play checkers."

They set up the game on a footstool between two chairs in the living room. Abe made the first move. Judith took her time deciding on her first move. Abe almost always won when they played checkers. Today she wanted to win.

A knock on the front door startled them both. Abe got up and pulled it open.

"Aunt Marcia! What are you doing here?"

Aunt Marcia was surrounded by her three children. Esther

was whimpering, and Anna was pouting. Richard charged past them into the living room without saying anything.

"What's wrong?" Judith asked.

"Oh, nothing's really wrong," Aunt Marcia said as she came into the living room and set Esther in a chair. "The children are a bit grumpy because we left the house in a hurry."

"What's the hurry?"

"Abe, is your mother here?" Aunt Marcia asked.

Abe shook his head. "She went shopping with Aunt Tina and Polly."

"Oh, dear," Aunt Marcia said. "I really need someone to look after the children for a couple hours. I completely forgot about a meeting at the church. I just remembered it twenty minutes ago, and I'm going to be late. I was hoping your mother would watch the children."

Abe and Judith looked at each other. They knew what was coming next.

"But of course the two of you are quite capable of caring for children," Aunt Marcia said. "I promise to be back as soon as possible."

Judith took a deep breath. "Of course, Aunt Marcia. You can leave the children with us."

"Oh, that's wonderful. I'll leave the meeting early and be back soon."

"Don't worry about it."

"Is Teddy here?" Richard asked.

"Yes, but he's sleeping."

"Let's wake him up."

"No!" Judith said firmly. She looked at Esther's droopy eyes. "Does Esther need a nap, too?"

Aunt Marcia nodded. "I'm afraid so. I don't think she will resist. She's very tired."

"We can use Polly's room," Abe said.

Aunt Marcia stooped to kiss the top of her children's heads.

"Good-bye, Esther, good-bye, Anna." She looked around. "Where's Richard?"

"He must have gone into the kitchen," Judith said. "I'll get them all a snack."

"I'd better get going," Aunt Marcia said. "Thank you very much for keeping the children."

"Enjoy your meeting," Judith said.

Abe closed the door behind Aunt Marcia. "Four children," he said. "We're playing nursemaid to four little children. This is worse than being restricted to the house."

"It won't be so bad," Judith said. "Teddy is already asleep, and Esther is about to fall over from exhaustion." She scooped up the two-year-old and cuddled her. "Just give Richard a book to look at, something with pictures."

Abe disappeared into the kitchen to look for Richard.

Four-year-old Anna crossed her arms across her chest and announced, "I didn't want to come here."

"We'll have a fun time," Judith assured her. "Do you want to help me put Esther down for a nap?"

"No. I want to go home."

"As soon as your mama comes back from her meeting."

Abe was back. "Richard is not in the kitchen."

Judith's stomach tightened. "Oh, no."

She looked up at the top of the stairs. Richard stood holding Teddy's hand.

"Teddy's awake," Richard announced.

"Richard Allerton, that was a naughty thing to do," Judith scolded.

"Play," Teddy said.

"No, nap time," Judith responded.

Esther started crying.

Anna flopped back into the sofa and screamed, "I want to go home."

"Teddy wants to see the lab," Richard said to Abe.

"No children in my lab!" Abe said loudly. "Upstairs, all of you. Everybody is going to take a nap."

"I'm too big for naps," Richard protested from the top of the stairs.

"I want to go home!" Anna wailed from the living room.

Teddy sat on the top step and bumped his way down the stairs.

"This is going to be a very long two hours," Abe said.

Judith sighed and started up the stairs with Esther.

CHAPTER 17

Disaster in the Kitchen

Of course Teddy and Esther did not go to sleep. With Richard in the house, sleeping was the last thing Teddy was willing to do. While Judith was in Abe's room trying to get Teddy to go to sleep, Richard lurked in the hallway hoping Teddy would come back out.

Esther would not stop crying. As long as Judith held her, Esther would merely whimper every few seconds. If Judith put her down, she howled with all the force her lungs could muster.

Finally Judith gave up trying to get the younger children to take naps. She went back downstairs with the toddlers in tow.

"I want to go home," Anna insisted loudly. She had not moved off the sofa.

"Do you want some juice?" Judith offered her, juggling Esther on one hip.

"I want to go home."

"You can play dress-up with Polly's clothes." Polly might not be pleased when she came home and found her things strewn around by a four-year-old, but Judith was desperate. Polly would have to understand. Anna loved playing dress-up with her cousins' clothes.

Anna thought about the offer for a moment. Just as Judith was feeling that she had solved this problem, Anna repeated, "I want to go home." She stuck out her bottom lip.

"Why do you want to go home?" Judith asked, trying not to sound as exasperated as she was.

"I want my mama."

"But your mama is not at home. She is at a meeting at church."

"I'm a big girl. I can be quiet for a meeting."

"I'm sure you could," Judith said patiently. "But there aren't any other children at the meeting. I'm sure your mama thought you would have more fun here."

"Mama was going to make cookies today."

So that was it, Judith thought. Aunt Marcia had promised to make cookies and then suddenly had remembered the meeting.

"Your mama will make cookies when she's finished with her meeting," Judith said.

Anna buried her face in the sofa cushion and refused to talk further.

Abe came into the room with Teddy on his shoulders and Richard close behind. He swung Teddy down and set him on the sofa next to Judith.

"These little ones are wearing me out," Abe said. "How much longer?"

"An hour and a half," Judith sighed.

Judith looked at all the children. Teddy and Esther would never admit how tired they were. Esther could hardly hold her eyes open. Teddy, while tired, was also excited to have his cousins around. Judith knew he wanted to play, but he was cranky, too. Anna only wanted to sulk over lost cookies. And Judith knew Richard would be bored in a few minutes. At six, he was the oldest of the younger set of cousins, and he tired of playing with the babies, as he called his sisters and Teddy. Judith calculated they had only a few minutes before the children would be out of control.

Structure, she thought. *Mama always says little children need structure.*

"Abe," Judith said, "maybe they need a snack. Mama always says Teddy gets cranky when he's hungry."

"It's worth a try. I could use a snack myself."

"Why?" Judith teased. "Are you feeling cranky?"

They headed for the kitchen. Abe went first with Richard.

"Come on, Teddy," Judith said. He refused to take her hand. But he followed her toward the kitchen, dragging his blanket and sucking his thumb.

Judith almost had Esther quieted down when she heard the crash behind her. She turned around just in time to see Teddy take a deep breath and start yelling. He had tripped over his own blanket and had landed on his stomach on the floor. Judith set Esther down so she could comfort Teddy. Esther immediately protested and started howling again.

"Abe!" Judith called. She hoped he would hear her over the two squalling toddlers. She picked up Esther again, then went to Teddy and sat on the floor. She put one child on each knee and patted their backs.

"Abe!"

He finally appeared. Esther was starting to settle down. Teddy was yelling as loud as ever.

Abe swooped Teddy up. "Let's leave the blanket here, buddy," Abe said. He twisted the corner of the blanket out of Teddy's fingers and hung it over the back of a dining room chair. Abe tickled

Teddy under one arm, and gradually Teddy's crying turned into giggling.

Esther rubbed her eyes with chubby fingers.

"She's so tired," Judith said. "But she won't sleep. I don't know what else to do."

"I got some bread and preserves out for a snack," Abe said. "Let's go back to that idea."

"Anna, do you want a snack?"

"I want to go home!"

Each carrying a weary toddler, Abe and Judith headed for the kitchen.

"Oh, no!"

"I fixed a snack," Richard announced proudly.

Twenty crookedly sliced pieces of bread were strewn around the kitchen table, each with a dab of strawberry preserves. More preserves were smeared across the table than on the bread. Now Richard was working on the honey jar. He swung a wooden spoon in circles in the air. As he made his proud announcement, drops of thick honey dribbled to the floor.

"Want some," Teddy said, and he wriggled out of Abe's arms. He headed straight for Richard. He stepped in the growing puddle of honey.

"Teddy! Don't move," Judith said. Instinctively she set Esther down so she could stop Teddy from tracking honey around the kitchen.

Esther screamed. Abe immediately picked her up. She kept screaming.

Judith snatched Teddy away from the honey and removed the wooden spoon from Richard's hand. She tossed it in the sink and turned back to Abe.

"She wants you," Abe said over Esther's howling.

They traded toddlers, and Esther quieted down again.

"Want some," Teddy repeated.

"All right, you can have some," Abe said. "You have to sit in

125

this chair. Don't climb out." He deposited Teddy in the chair at the head of the table.

"Want some." Teddy reached out and grabbed four slices of bread. He licked the preserves off one slice and then started on the next one.

With Esther on one hip, Judith snatched away Teddy's extra bread. "You have to eat the whole thing," Judith said. "You can't just lick the preserves off."

"Want some! Want some!" Teddy clamored for another taste of the sweetened preserves.

Richard had found a table knife and was smearing honey on another piece of bread.

"Abe, stop him," urged Judith.

Abe gently pried the knife out of Richard's hand. "I think we've got enough snack now, Richard."

Richard climbed into a chair and reached for a piece of bread. Judith handed one to Esther, still in her arms. For a moment everything was quiet.

Judith sighed heavily and looked at Abe. "They've destroyed the kitchen. We can't let your mother come home and find it like this."

"I know," Abe said, starting to gather stray scraps of bread. "I'll clean it up, if you can keep an eye on the kids." He moved to the sink in search of a rag.

Esther finished her bread and seemed more content.

"I'm going to check on Anna," Judith said. She turned to go back to the living room.

Anna had finally moved off the sofa. Now she sat on top of the checkerboard on the footstool. Checkers were scattered around the room. Mustering up her patience, Judith knelt in front of Anna.

"Anna, what's wrong?" Judith asked.

"I wanted to go to the meeting, but Mama wouldn't let me," Anna blurted. Anna's bottom lip was hanging out, but at least she was looking at Judith now.

"Are you sure you wouldn't like to play dress-up with Polly's clothes?"

This time Anna nodded.

"Okay," Judith said. "Maybe that will cheer Esther up, too."

They started for the stairs.

Abe burst out of the kitchen. "Richard and Teddy got out the back door."

"Well, go get them!" Judith changed directions and headed for the kitchen and the back door.

"I want to play dress-up," Anna said.

"Yes, we will," Judith promised. "We just have to see if the boys are all right."

Outside, when Abe started running for Teddy, the little boy thought it was a game. Giggling, he ran even faster.

Richard was headed for the lab.

"Stay away from my lab!" Abe called after him.

Richard stopped, turned around, and stomped his foot.

Abe finally caught up with Teddy, picked him up, and turned his attention to Richard.

"We can play outside for a while," Abe said, "but you have to stay out of the lab."

Richard was not happy about this restriction, but he did not protest further.

"I play," Esther said, and she wriggled to get free of Judith. Judith gladly let her go. Anna had already forgotten about playing dress-up and was chasing Richard in circles. Abe put Teddy down again, with a warning to stay away from the lab. He and Judith collapsed on the back step.

The day was a nice one for the middle of May, but still a bit breezy.

"They probably should have coats on," Judith observed. But she made no move to get the coats.

Abe shrugged. "As long as they keep moving, they won't get cold."

"Did you get the kitchen cleaned up?"

"Most of it. It's hard to get honey off the floor. I'll have to mop the whole floor, I think."

Judith groaned. "What time is it?"

Abe told her.

"One more hour, maybe less," Judith said optimistically. "They all said they would be back in a couple of hours, and they've already been gone more than an hour."

The children were all happy, at least for the moment. The deep backyard was a good place for them to spill out their energy—as long as they stayed away from the lab. Squealing with delight, they chased each other around the yard. Every now and then, they collapsed in a heap of flailing arms and legs. Judith decided just to let the children play outside until they wore themselves out enough to be quiet in the house. Maybe Teddy and Esther would even fall asleep.

Judith dared to close her eyes and lift her face to the spring sun. Summer was coming soon. Every year, after a cold, harsh Minnesota winter, Judith looked forward to the summer. She wanted the hot lazy days to blot out the memory of how cold her toes had been for the last few months.

Teddy's screams shattered the peacefulness.

Chapter 18
Trapped!

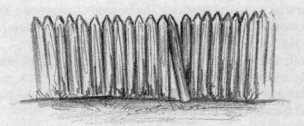

Judith scrambled off the step with Abe right behind her. At the far end of the yard, the children huddled around Teddy. Judith could not see what was making him scream. But she knew it was not a scream of protest. Something was hurting her little brother. She hurtled herself across the yard. For a change, she was three steps ahead of Abe instead of behind him.

When she got there, Judith gasped. "How did this happen?"

But of course the children were too young to answer her question. Somehow, Teddy had gotten his head caught between two loose boards in the fence. All Judith could see was the back of his denim overalls—and the rough board cutting into his tiny neck. The vein in the side of his neck popped out further with every scream.

Esther started crying again. Hers was a cry of anxiety. As much as she hated to do it, Judith would have to let Esther cry while she concentrated on helping Teddy.

"How in the world did he do that?" Abe asked loudly.

"I guess he was curious," Judith snapped. "We have to get him out."

Judith knelt next to Teddy, who had not stopped screaming. She did not blame him. She was not sure she would be able to stop screaming if she had her head stuck in a fence. She held on to Teddy's waist.

"Teddy, we're going to get you out."

Abe was trying to separate the boards that trapped Teddy.

"It won't budge," Abe said, after several attempts. "Try pulling his head out."

Judith stuck her hand through the fence and grabbed the top of Teddy's head. Ignoring his screams, she pulled back gently. His head was just too big. She could not imagine how he had gotten his head through the opening in the first place.

"His head won't come out," she said emphatically. "We have to get that board off. Keep pulling on it. At least you're keeping the pressure off his neck."

Anna tugged on Judith's sleeve. "Richard's in the lab," she tattled.

Judith threw a glance at Abe. "Do you have anything out in the lab that is dangerous?"

"The copper coil and the glass beakers are out on the workbench."

"Don't let go of that board!" Judith said. "I'll get Richard."

She pulled her arm back through the fence and flew across the yard toward the lab. Opening the door, she saw that Richard had pushed the barrel up against the workbench and climbed on top of it. He was on his knees, leaning over the workbench. In one hand was a beaker, and in the other hand a coil of copper wiring. When he saw her, he looked startled.

"Richard Daniel Allerton, that's the second naughty thing you've done today. We've told you a thousand times not to play in here."

"I'm not playing. I'm working like Abe."

"We'll talk about that later." Judith snatched Richard off the barrel and pushed open the little door. He thrashed for his freedom, but she tightened her grip. The last thing she wanted was another emergency. She carried him all the way to the back fence and set him firmly on the ground.

"Stay right there!" she demanded. "Anna, you, too. And Esther."

Esther was still crying, but Judith ignored her. She took the toddler, lined her up against the fence with her siblings, and turned her attention back to her own little brother.

Abe had managed to loosen the fence board a bit more, but it still would not come free.

"Keep pulling, Abe," Judith urged. "We have to figure this out. We need a plan."

"I don't know what else to try," Abe said, pulling on the board in vain.

"That board has to come off," Judith insisted. She was starting to panic. "And you're stronger than I am."

"I can't think straight with all this noise!"

Now Anna had started crying, too.

"What seems to be the problem?"

Judith whirled around to see Uncle Enoch standing behind them. She had not heard his shuffle in the grass above the noise coming from Teddy and Esther and her own worry about what to do next. But she was enormously relieved to see him.

"Uncle Enoch, Teddy is stuck."

"One minute they were playing, and the next minute he was screaming," Abe said.

"Where is his mother?" Uncle Enoch asked. Awkwardly, he kneeled down on his good leg and put his hand soothingly on

Teddy's back. Surprisingly, Teddy's screams seemed a little less loud.

"Mama and Aunt Tina went downtown," explained Judith. "They left us in charge of Teddy."

"And the others?" Uncle Enoch gestured toward the Allerton children.

"Aunt Marcia had a meeting. She is supposed to be back soon."

"Let's see what we can do for Teddy," Uncle Enoch said. His voice was low and even. Judith wondered if Uncle Enoch felt as calm as he sounded. "I assume you've already tried pulling the board back."

"It won't go back far enough," Abe said.

"Then it will have to come off," his father said.

"That's what I said," Judith declared.

"Maybe if we pull on it together—"

Uncle Enoch shook his head. "No, Abe, let's do it the right way. Teddy is in no immediate threat of harm. Let's be careful to be sure no one gets hurt."

"What should we do, Uncle Enoch?" Judith asked.

"Abe," Uncle Enoch said, "go to my toolshed. There is a large claw hammer hanging just inside the door, to the left. Bring that and the small hand saw."

Abe shot across the yard.

Uncle Enoch kept his large hand on Teddy's little back. "We're going to get you out, Teddy. Just hold still. Don't wiggle around. Abe will be right back with the tools we need to take the fence apart."

Teddy's shoulders heaved in a silent sob, but the screaming had stopped.

Judith looked at the Allerton children. They stood motionless against the fence where she had left them. Esther was not crying, but she had half of one fist stuffed in her mouth. White-faced, they watched Uncle Enoch in action.

Abe was back with the tools.

"We're going to try to take just one board out of the fence," Uncle Enoch explained. "If that doesn't work, we'll use the saw to cut a bigger opening so we can get Teddy's head out."

Judith nodded. Uncle Enoch had a plan. He even had a second plan in case the first one did not work. She felt comforted by his methodical approach.

"Judith," Uncle Enoch said as he pulled himself to a standing position again, "you come down here with Teddy. Keep him very still. Don't let him try to turn his head."

"Yes, Uncle Enoch." Judith got into position beside Teddy. With one hand she rubbed his back, and with the other she held his head steady.

"Teddy out!" he said. It was the first time he had spoken words since sticking his head through the fence. Judith was encouraged.

"Yes," she said, "Teddy will get out."

"Abe, you hang on to the fence board," Uncle Enoch said. "We don't want it to fly out of control and hurt someone when I get the last nail out."

"Yes, Papa." Abe gripped the board, one hand at the top, the other along the side near Teddy's head.

Slowly, carefully, Uncle Enoch pulled out the four nails that held the board in place. Then he pulled on the board. It did not come loose.

"Will we have to use the saw?" Judith asked anxiously.

"I don't think so. Just keep his head still."

Not once during the whole episode had Uncle Enoch sounded upset. He just concentrated on what he needed to do.

"Abe, help me," Uncle Enoch said. "Pull on the bottom while I pull on the top."

The board came loose. Teddy was free.

The little boy buried his face in his sister's skirt. Except for scratches along the side of his face and neck, he was all right. He would have some bruises for a few days, but he was not seriously hurt.

"No play," he said quietly.

"No, Teddy, you don't have to play," Judith said. She picked him up and held him close to her chest. How small he seemed! "Shhh. Just rest."

"He looks like he'll be fine," Uncle Enoch said.

"Thank you, Uncle Enoch. I don't know how I let this happen, but I'm glad you came along when you did."

"Don't blame yourself," Uncle Enoch said. "I remember when you and Abe were this age. You could get yourselves into trouble faster than any of us could say your names."

His eyes twinkled. "As a matter of fact, you still get into trouble, or you wouldn't have been home minding four small children on a Saturday afternoon."

Judith glanced at Abe. Compared to what might have happened to Teddy, their punishment did not seem so harsh anymore.

Judith cradled Teddy, who now looked like he was ready to surrender to sleep.

Abe picked up the hammer and saw. "Thank you, Papa. You knew just what to do."

"You were doing fine, Abe," Uncle Enoch said. "You knew you needed to get that board off. You just needed to slow down a little bit and think the problem through so you could do it safely."

Abe nodded.

Uncle Enoch looked at Teddy asleep in Judith's arms. "I would hate to think of anything happening to Teddy. If we had a telephone, and an emergency like this happened, you could call for help."

Abe's face showed his surprise. "A telephone? Really?"

They started walking toward the house. "I'll talk to your mother and see what she thinks," Uncle Enoch said. "But you must understand that the telephone will not be a toy. It is a tool—like this hammer and saw—to use in an emergency."

"Yes, Papa."

Judith carried Teddy. The Allerton children straggled behind her.

Inside the kitchen, Uncle Enoch crossed to the sink to wash his hands. His shoe stuck.

"What is this?" he asked. "Why is the floor sticky?"

"I made a snack," Richard explained.

Judith rolled her eyes. Abe went to get the mop.

CHAPTER 19

The New Phone

"We've waited a long time for this day," Uncle Enoch said.

Judith smiled at the excitement she saw in Abe's eyes.

"I didn't think this day would really come," Abe said. "By this afternoon, we'll have a telephone in our house."

The three of them stood outside the Stevenson home, watching the man from the telephone company sitting atop the pole behind the house. Several families in the neighborhood had requested telephones. By the time the man was finished with his day's work, they would all have them.

"When you said you would think about getting a telephone," Abe said to his father, "I didn't expect it would happen quite this soon."

"It's been five months since the day Teddy got stuck in the fence," Judith reminded her cousin.

"We haven't had any emergencies during that time," Abe said, "but we might have."

"Next time we'll be prepared," Uncle Enoch said.

Judith studied her uncle. Even in getting a telephone, Enoch Stevenson had been methodical and organized. Many Minneapolis residents had talked about getting a telephone. Abe's father had actually done it.

The phone in the Fisk house had been installed two weeks earlier. Judith's parents were waiting for friends and family to get telephones, too.

The summer had flown by. Judith hardly got to sit and enjoy the sun. Her mother had kept her busy in the garden and watching Teddy. In the evenings, though, she and Abe had often wandered the streets downtown amid the new electric lights. Their midnight escapade had become another humorous story added to the family's collection. Judith was sure Teddy and the other cousins would grow up hearing about it.

Now the summer days were waning once again. Fall would sneak up and overpower summer any day now. Teddy would soon be two years old. No one thought of him as a baby anymore. He was an energetic little boy. Abe and Judith would turn thirteen in a few weeks. The crack was gone from Abe's voice. In the last year, he had grown to be a full six inches taller than Judith.

"I'd better go see if your mother needs any help," Uncle Enoch said. He left Judith and Abe alone watching the telephone man.

"Look at all those wires," Abe said. "They go to the next block, and the block after that. Someday they'll stretch to Chicago, Washington, and New York. I feel like I'm connected to the whole world. The telephone will make that come true."

"Do you know anyone in New York or Chicago to call?" Judith asked.

"That's not the point," Abe said. "I could call if I wanted to."

"We could call Cincinnati," Judith suggested, "and talk to Uncle David and Aunt Daria."

"See? There are lots of places to call."

"My father says the same thing about the railroad—about being connected, I mean. He says the railroad will connect the whole country, from the Atlantic to the Pacific."

"Is he going to the parade today?" Abe asked.

"Of course! He wouldn't miss a parade celebrating the Great Northern's connection through Minneapolis. Someday he wants to ride that line all the way to the West Coast."

"I hope the telephone is installed in time to go to the parade," Abe said. "I don't want to have to choose between the two."

"Papa is talking about getting electricity in our house, too," Judith said. "The railroad office is going to have it soon. Dr. Dan's clinic already has it."

"My father is not quite convinced about electricity," Abe reported. "And he's not sure that Jim Hill will be able to run the railroad at a profit, either."

Judith shrugged one shoulder. "He changed his mind about a telephone. He might change his mind about those things, too."

"But he might be right," Abe said. "Other railroads have run out of money. What if Jim Hill does, too?"

Judith could not hide her amusement.

"What's so funny?" Abe asked.

"You! You sound almost as cautious as your father."

"It's not good to rush into everything. I just hope Jim Hill has a good plan."

Judith giggled. She couldn't help it.

"Judith!" Aunt Tina called. She came around the side of the house and stood with them. "Did you bring your sampler? Your father told me that he made a frame for it."

"Yes, it's in the kitchen."

They went in the house, and Judith removed the brown wrapping paper that protected her finished sampler. Five stanzas of the hymn were neatly stitched beneath the glass.

Children of the heavenly Father,
Safely in His bosom gather;
Nestling bird nor star in heaven
Such a refuge e'er was given.

God His own doth tend and nourish,
In His holy courts they flourish;
From all evil things He spares them,
In His mighty arms He bears them.

Neither life nor death shall ever
From the Lord His children sever;
Unto them His grace He showeth,
And their sorrows all He knoweth.

Praise the Lord in joyful numbers,
Your Protector never slumbers;
At the will of your Defender
Every foeman must surrender.

Though He giveth or He taketh,
God His children ne'er forsaketh;
His the loving purpose solely
To preserve them pure and holy.

"You've done a beautiful job," Aunt Tina said, "and it's my—"

"I know, your favorite hymn."

Aunt Tina smiled. "Have I said that before?"

Judith nodded. "You, and Mama, and Aunt Alison. Did you

have a meeting and choose a favorite hymn together?"

Aunt Tina laughed. "No, nothing like that. We've just all experienced the special care of the heavenly Father. We know what it means to be His children. Why did you choose this hymn to stitch?"

Judith thought for a moment. "I guess I like it, too. It tells me all the things that a good parent should be."

"The perfect parent," Aunt Tina emphasized, "the heavenly parent."

Abe burst through the back door. "He says it's ready, it's ready. We can try to make a call."

He led the way to his father's study, where the phone was. Judith and Aunt Tina followed.

"Who should we call?" Aunt Tina asked. "We must call someone to try out the line to be sure it works."

"Let's let Abe decide who to call," Uncle Enoch said. "After all, if it were not for his pestering, we wouldn't even have a telephone."

"Well," said Abe, "I have been wondering if Uncle Charles wants to meet me somewhere to watch the parade today."

"Call him!" Aunt Tina said. She picked up the phone and handed it to Abe.

Nervously, Abe wound the handle and jangled the bell. The operator came on and he asked for the Fisk house.

"Hello?"

"Uncle Charles? Is that you?"

"Abe! Hello! I see your telephone is working now."

"And so is yours."

"Is this your first call?"

"Yes. Uncle Charles, I wanted to know if you would like to meet me to watch the parade together."

"Certainly. I'll meet you at the corner of Washington and Hennepin in thirty minutes."

"Great!"

140

"Make sure Judith comes along. I don't want her to miss this."

Abe glanced at Judith. "I'll bring her. I promise."

"See you then."

They hung up.

"What did it sound like?" Aunt Tina wanted to know.

"It sounded like his voice," Abe said, "but a little scratchy."

"Did you have any trouble understanding him?" Judith asked.

Abe shook his head. "No, it was perfect communication. He'll meet us in thirty minutes. He wants to be sure you come."

Judith smiled.

The phone rang. Everyone jumped.

Aunt Tina laughed. "I wondered what it would sound like to get a call."

Gingerly, she picked up the earpiece and spoke into the mouthpiece. "Hello?"

"Tina? It's Charles."

"Hello, Charles. Did you forget something?"

"Yes. I forgot Teddy. He wants to talk on the phone."

"Put him on."

"I talk phone," said a little voice.

Aunt Tina smiled broadly. "Yes, Teddy, you are talking on the phone."

"Bye." Teddy was finished with the phone.

"Can you imagine," Abe said, "that Teddy will not remember when there was no telephone in the house?"

"We'll have to remind him about how he talked on the phone the very first day we had one," Judith said.

"Another family story," Aunt Tina said.

"We'd better get going," Abe said. "We don't want to be late meeting your father."

When Judith and Abe reached the corner of Hennepin and Washington, the street was swarming with onlookers. But Papa was there, exactly where he had said he would be. The three of them strolled down to Bridge Square and squeezed themselves into a place where they could see fairly well.

Thousands of people poured out into the streets. Long before the parade began, the avenues were thick with curious railroad fans. Jim Hill had achieved his success in Minneapolis, and the whole city—except perhaps Uncle Enoch—seemed eager to congratulate him.

The stone arch bridge curved magnificently across the river in front of the Pillsbury A mill. A locomotive thick with soot chugged across the bridge ahead of a string of freight cars. The best flour in the country was on its way to the western states.

"The telephone and the railroad, all in one day," Papa said. "What a celebration."

"It's not a celebration of the telephone or the railroad," Abe said. "Not even electricity."

"No?"

"It's a celebration of the future," Abe said. "Minneapolis will be changed. The country will not be the same after this. The people are celebrating the future."

Yes, thought Judith, *they are. And so am I.*

There's More!

The American Adventure continues with *The Streetcar Riots*. On their way to Easter dinner at their aunt and uncle's home, Richard and Anna Allerton find themselves in the middle of a riot. The streetcar drivers are on strike, and thousands of people fill the streets. Angry words grow louder, and suddenly a group of men overturns a streetcar. Richard and Anna are separated from the rest of their family. How will they manage to get home safely? And when this latest outbreak of violence between workers and business owners only makes Uncle Charles and Uncle Enoch that much angrier at each other, what can the family do to settle its differences?

You're in for the ultimate
American Adventure!
Collect all 48 books!